BOUND BY SECRETS

THE PAGES AND PAWS MYSTERY SERIES
BOOK 2

POPPY BRIDGEMAN

Ebook ISBN: 978-1-990509-65-0
Paperback ISBN: 978-1-990509-64-3

Cover created by Getcovers

FREE BOOK

Claim your copy of The Charleston Diary when you sign up for my newsletter. Learn how Ginny solved a case of forgery before she headed to the peace and tranquility of Tidehaven Cove.

1

The morning of the Tidehaven Cove Literary Fair dawned crisp and bright, with just enough autumn bite in the air to make browsing book stalls seem like the perfect activity. I stood in the doorway of Hampton Books, coffee mug in hand, watching volunteers transform the village green into a literary wonderland. At my feet, Austen and Hardy sat alert and watchful, their corgi ears perked at every new sound and movement across the green.

"Nervous?" Malcolm asked, appearing beside me with his usual punctuality. Even at seven in the morning, his bow tie was perfectly straight and his white hair neatly combed. His tone was polite but formal. The same courtesy he'd maintained since I'd inherited the shop.

"Terrified," I admitted, taking another sip of coffee. "What if no one comes? What if the weather turns? What if —"

"What if you stop borrowing trouble and start enjoying the fact that you've organized the most ambitious literary event Tidehaven has seen in decades?" Freya interrupted, bounding down the stairs from the apartment with her usual morning energy. Her curly hair was barely contained in a messy bun, and she'd somehow managed to get book dust on her sweater before breakfast.

Hardy immediately trotted over to greet her, while Austen sniffed the corners of the shop. I hoped it was not a hint that we had vermin. Though I supposed having Captain roaming around whenever it pleased him kept mice away.

"Easy for you to say," I replied. "You're not the one who convinced the village council to let us take over half the town for three days."

Through the window, I could see Oliver Blackthorn unlocking his antique shop with obvious reluctance. He'd agreed to host one of the writing workshops in his back room, but only after I'd promised that "literary types" wouldn't damage his precious inventory. The fact that he was still hoping to buy my bookshop probably influenced his cooperation, though he'd never admit it.

"The setup's going beautifully," Malcolm observed, nodding toward the green where volunteers were arranging book stalls in neat rows. "Mrs. Wong's design for the layout is quite ingenious."

Lily Wong, who ran the village art gallery, had volunteered to coordinate the fair's visual elements. Her eye for spacing and flow had transformed my rough sketches into something that actually looked professional. Right now she was directing the placement of the small stage where authors would give readings, her slight frame and precise gestures commanding surprising authority.

"There's our first author arrival," Freya announced, pointing toward a modest blue car pulling up near the village hall.

Both dogs immediately perked up, their tails wagging as they sensed the excitement in the air.

A woman emerged from the car, tall and elegant with silver-streaked hair swept into a sophisticated updo. Even from a distance, she carried herself with the confidence of someone accustomed to public speaking. Diana Hartwell, bestselling thriller novelist and our weekend's featured guest author.

"She looks exactly like her book jacket photos," Freya said admiringly. "Though I suppose that's the point."

Diana was followed by a younger woman, presumably her assistant, who immediately began unloading boxes of books from the car's boot. The assistant was short and curvy with bright purple hair that definitely hadn't come from nature, wearing a vintage dress that somehow managed to look both professional and quirky.

"I should go greet her," I said, setting down my coffee mug. "First impressions and all that."

"Take these," Malcolm said, producing a folder from seemingly nowhere. "Final schedules, room assignments, and the list of dietary restrictions for the catered lunch."

I'd learned not to question Malcolm's organizational abilities. Somehow he always had exactly the right information at exactly the right moment, as if he maintained a mystical connection to all things administrative.

"Come on, you two," I said to the dogs, who immediately fell into step beside me. Walking across the green with my canine escorts, I could feel the familiar flutter of pre-event nerves mixed with genuine excitement. When I'd inherited Hampton Books eight months ago, I'd never imagined myself organizing literary festivals. But Tidehaven Cove had embraced me as one of their own, and this fair felt like my way of giving something back to the community that had become my home.

"Ms. Hartwell?" I called as I approached. "I'm Ginny Hampton from Hampton Books. Welcome to Tidehaven Cove."

Diana turned with a practiced smile that seemed genuinely warm. "Miss Hampton! How lovely to finally meet you. Your emails were so thorough. I feel like I already know the village."

Hardy immediately approached Diana with his tail wagging, and she bent down to give him a proper greeting. "And who are these handsome fellows?"

"That's Hardy being friendly, and this is Austen sticking to me like a bur," I said. "Please, call me Ginny. And you must be..." I turned to the assistant.

"Priya Patel," the young woman said, extending a hand with a firm grip. "I handle Diana's schedule, social media, and anything else that needs handling. Though I have to say, your organization has been impeccable. Most events are chaos until the last minute."

"Don't jinx it," I laughed. "We've still got three days to go."

As we chatted about logistics and timing, I noticed another car arriving—this one considerably less modest than Diana's. A sleek black sedan deposited a sharp-looking woman in an expensive suit who immediately began surveying the setup with calculating eyes.

"That'll be Sarah Pemberton," Diana observed, following my gaze. "Literary agent extraordinaire. Lovely woman, but she doesn't suffer fools gladly."

"Good to know," I said, making a mental note to be extra careful around Ms. Pemberton. "She's here for the 'meet the agent' sessions?"

"Among other things. Sarah's always scouting for new talent, though she's quite selective." Diana's tone suggested this was both praise and warning.

The morning continued with a steady stream of arrivals. Marcus Webb from Moorland Press arrived in a battered estate car that looked like it had seen better decades, his rumpled appearance contrasting sharply with Sarah Pemberton's polished professionalism. Romance novelist Colin Mitchell, writing as Scarlett Fox, pulled up in a sensible Honda, looking comfortable and unassuming despite his success.

Both dogs greeted each new arrival with interest, tails wagging and hopeful of treats. It was amusing to watch their different personalities both with the same aim, but Hardy's tactic was overwhelm with love, Austen sniffed and judged.

By nine o'clock, the green was bustling with activity. Local volunteers arranged book displays while visiting authors and industry professionals examined their assigned spaces. The atmosphere was friendly and collaborative, with the kind of excited energy that comes from bringing book lovers together.

That's when Gary Stephens arrived.

The dented white Ford that pulled up near the tea shop disgorged a thin, slightly hunched figure who immediately began surveying the scene with obvious dissatisfaction. Even from across the green, there was something off-putting about his posture—aggressive and defensive at the same time.

Both dogs reacted immediately. Austen's ears flattened slightly, and she moved closer to my leg, while Hardy's usually cheerful demeanor shifted to alert wariness. They'd both sensed something troubling about this newcomer.

"Oh dear," Diana murmured beside me. "That's Gary Stephens. I was rather hoping he wouldn't show up."

"You know him?"

"Know of him. He's been... persistent... at various industry events. Calls himself Blake Savage when he's pitching his political thriller." Her tone was diplomatically neutral, but something in her expression suggested she'd had unpleasant experiences with Mr. Stephens.

As if summoned by our conversation, Gary spotted our little group and began making his way over. His walk was purposeful and slightly aggressive, someone who expected resistance and was prepared to push through it. Both dogs pressed closer to me, their protective instincts clearly activated.

"Ms. Hartwell!" he called out while still twenty feet away. "Thank goodness you're here. Finally, someone who understands what we're up against."

"Mr. Stephens," Diana replied with professional politeness. "How nice to see you again."

Gary was thin to the point of appearing gaunt, with lank brown hair and clothes that hung on him as if he'd recently lost weight. His eyes had an intense quality that made me instinctively step closer to Diana, while Austen positioned herself between Gary and me with quiet determination.

"I don't believe we've met," I interjected, extending my hand. "Ginny Hampton, event coordinator."

His handshake was surprisingly strong for someone so slight, but his attention had already returned to Diana. "Ms. Hartwell, as someone who's succeeded in the thriller market, surely you've noticed how publishers are becoming more risk-averse about political content? They're terrified of literature that exposes real governmental corruption."

Hardy had retreated to stand beside Austen, both dogs

watching Gary with the same focused attention they gave to every slug and spider in the garden.

"Publishers face many considerations when selecting manuscripts," Diana replied diplomatically. "Market conditions, reader interest, production costs —"

"Market conditions!" Gary's voice rose enough to draw glances from nearby fairgoers. "That's exactly what they told me about my political thriller. 'Current market conditions don't favor conspiracy-focused narratives.' As if truth-telling about institutional corruption is a matter of fashion trends!"

"Perhaps we should discuss this at a more appropriate time," Diana suggested gently. "Miss Hampton has a great deal to coordinate this morning."

"Of course, of course," Gary said, though his expression suggested he considered this a mere postponement rather than a dismissal. "But surely you agree that someone needs to challenge the industry's cowardice about publishing work that matters? Literature that exposes the kind of truths that make establishment figures uncomfortable?"

After he wandered off toward the book stalls, both dogs visibly relaxed, though they continued to track his movement across the green with watchful eyes.

"Well," Priya said finally, "this weekend just got interesting."

Diana gave me an apologetic look. "I probably should have warned you about Gary when you sent the attendee list. He's... intense about his theories."

"Theories?" I asked, though Gary's brief conversation had made his world-view fairly clear.

"Gary believes there's an organized conspiracy in publishing to suppress political thrillers that reveal 'uncomfortable truths' about government corruption," Diana explained. "He's convinced that his manuscript is being rejected not for quality issues, but because it's too dangerous for publishers to handle."

I watched Gary cornering one of the volunteer book-sellers, gesticulating animatedly while the poor woman looked around desperately for rescue. Even from a distance, I could see the intensity that had made both dogs uneasy.

"How often does he turn up at these events?" I asked.

"More often than anyone would like," Diana replied. "He considers himself a warrior in a world of literary cowards. Unfortunately, his passion for his theories far exceeds his actual writing ability."

"Right," I said with determined cheerfulness, while Austen and Hardy settled at my feet, apparently having decided that Diana was trustworthy. "Let's get you settled in. Your reading isn't until this afternoon, so you'll have time to explore the village before then."

As we headed toward the village hall where authors were checking in, I caught sight of Malcolm standing in the bookshop doorway, watching Gary's animated conversation with obvious concern. When our eyes met, he raised an eyebrow in a look that clearly said, "This one's going to be trouble."

I had no idea how right he was.

The Tidehaven Cove Literary Fair was officially under-way, and already I could sense undercurrents of tension that had nothing to do with event logistics. Looking around at the beautiful morning setup. Book stalls gleaming in the sunshine, authors chatting with early visitors, the smell of fresh pastries drifting from Elspeth's tea shop—I tried to focus on the positive.

After all, what could possibly go wrong at a peaceful village book fair?

2

———————

By ten o'clock, the Tidehaven Cove Literary Fair was in full swing. The village green buzzed with visitors browsing book stalls, children clutching new purchases, and the pleasant hum of literary conversation. From my vantage point near the information booth, I could see everything was proceeding exactly as planned.

Well, almost everything. Austen and Hardy flanked me like furry sentries, both dogs maintaining their unusual alertness since Gary's arrival.

"Miss Hampton!" The sharp voice cut through the morning chatter like a knife through butter. "We need to discuss the scheduling conflict immediately."

I turned to find Sarah Pemberton striding toward me with determined efficiency. In person, she was even more formidable than I'd imagined, steel-gray hair in a perfect bob, designer glasses that probably cost more than my monthly rent back in Charleston, and a leather portfolio clutched like a weapon.

Both dogs immediately perked up at her approach, but

their reaction was entirely different from their wariness around Gary. Hardy's tail began a tentative wag, while Austen tilted her head like she was waiting to decide on this human's worthiness.

"Good morning, Ms. Pemberton," I said, consulting my clipboard. "What seems to be the problem?"

"The 'meet the agent' sessions are scheduled opposite Colin Mitchell's signing. Half my potential attendees will be queuing for romance novels instead of learning about proper submission protocols." Her tone suggested this was tantamount to literary vandalism.

Before I could respond, a harried-looking woman with short black hair and paint-stained fingers rushed up to us. "Ginny, thank goodness. We've got a situation with the children's story corner—"

"Jamal, meet Sarah Pemberton," I said quickly. "Sarah, this is Jamal Rahman from the village primary school. She's coordinating our young readers' program."

"Pleasure," Sarah said crisply, though her attention remained fixed on the scheduling crisis. "About those sessions—"

"Actually," I interrupted, "having Colin's signing at the same time might work perfectly. People waiting in his queue could learn about the submission process. Cross-pollination of audiences and all that."

Sarah considered this, like she was evaluating a business proposal. "Hmm. That's actually rather clever. Romance readers looking to try their hand at writing..."

"Exactly. Now, Jamal, what's happening with the story corner?"

"Gary Stephens," Jamal said grimly. "He's 'observing' the children's event, making loud comments about how modern children's literature lacks proper educational value. The volunteer reader is completely flustered, and some parents are starting to look annoyed."

Through the crowd, I could see Gary standing at the edge of the small crowd gathered around the story corner, arms crossed and expression disapproving. Even from a distance, his body language radiated criticism. Both dogs immediately swiveled their attention in that direction, Hardy's ears twitching slightly.

"I'll handle it," I said, already heading in that direction. "Sarah, could you take a look at the afternoon schedule? I'd value your input on the flow."

Sarah actually smiled at that. Apparently professional consultation was the key to her cooperation. "Of course. I have several suggestions for improvement."

The story corner was set up near the ancient oak tree that dominated one corner of the green, with colorful cushions arranged in a semicircle. About fifteen children aged five to ten sat cross-legged, listening to Mrs. Fairweather from the village library read from a picture book about a dragon who was afraid of the dark.

Gary stood just outside the circle, muttering comments like "Complete nonsense" and "No wonder children can't read properly these days" in a voice just loud enough to be disruptive. Austen and Hardy followed me closely, staying near my legs as we approached Gary.

"Mr. Stephens," I said pleasantly, approaching with my best event coordinator smile. "How are you enjoying the fair so far?"

He turned toward me with intense focus, like he'd been waiting for an audience. "Miss Hampton, isn't it? I have to say, I'm rather disappointed in the caliber of literature being promoted here. That dragon story, for instance—pure fantasy with no educational merit whatsoever."

I suppressed the urge to point out that most parents weren't eager to return to Victorian-era moral tales about children who died from disobedience.

"Children tend to enjoy stories that spark their imagination," I replied diplomatically. "Different audiences, different needs."

"But that's exactly the problem with modern publishing!" Gary's voice rose enough that several parents turned to look at us, their expressions shifting from mild curiosity to concern. "Everything's dumbed down for mass appeal instead of challenging readers to think. Literature should educate, should prepare children for the real threats they'll face as adults—government corruption, institutional conspiracy, the systematic suppression of truth by those in power."

"Perhaps we could discuss your concerns somewhere less disruptive to the children's event?" I suggested, gently guiding him away from the story circle while the dogs remained protectively close.

"Certainly, certainly. Though I hope you understand that what we're witnessing here is part of a larger pattern— the deliberate dumbing-down of readers to make them more susceptible to propaganda and less likely to question authority."

As we walked, I noticed Colin Mitchell setting up at his signing table near the tea shop. He was arranging copies of his latest Scarlett Fox romance novel, Passion's Promise. A small queue was already forming, mostly women of various ages clutching well-worn paperbacks.

"Look at that," Gary said with obvious disgust. "Pure

commercial manipulation. Romance novels condition readers to accept simplified emotional responses instead of grappling with complex political realities."

I glanced at Colin to see if he'd overheard, but he was chatting pleasantly with a fan about whether the next book in his series would feature the same hero. His expression was friendly and professional, giving no sign he'd noticed Gary's commentary.

"Romance is actually one of the strongest-selling genres," I pointed out. "Clearly it serves a need for readers."

"A need for escapism, perhaps. But what about literature that challenges, that forces people to confront uncomfortable truths?" Gary's eyes gleamed with familiar fervor. "My political thriller exposes the kind of governmental conspiracy that publishers refuse to acknowledge exists."

We'd reached the information booth, where Malcolm was efficiently directing visitors toward their areas of interest. He took one look at Gary's animated expression and my slightly strained smile, then smoothly intervened.

"Mr. Stephens, I believe you mentioned an interest in our workshop on research techniques for historical fiction? It begins in twenty minutes in the village hall."

"Research techniques?" Gary's interest was immediate but suspicious. "What kind of research? I hope it's not another session on 'making things believable for mass audiences' instead of pursuing actual truth."

"The workshop focuses on authenticating source materials and verifying historical claims," Malcolm replied with diplomatic precision. "I believe you'll find it quite... thorough."

"Excellent. Though I should warn you, my own research methods are probably more advanced than what most amateur historians attempt. When you're exposing real conspiracy, you can't rely on conventional academic sources —they're all compromised by institutional bias."

After Gary headed off toward the village hall, Malcolm turned to me with raised eyebrows. "Challenging morning?"

"You could say that. He's already disrupted the children's story time and criticized Colin's romance novels loud enough for half the green to hear." I consulted my clipboard again, while both dogs settled into more relaxed positions now that Gary had moved away. "Please tell me the rest of the attendees are less... intense."

"Most are perfectly lovely," Malcolm assured me. "Though I did notice Ms. Pemberton had rather sharp words with the coffee volunteer about the difference between espresso and filter coffee."

"At least that's a solvable problem." I looked around the bustling fair, trying to recapture the morning's optimistic energy. "How are book sales going?"

"Quite well, actually. The local history section is particularly popular, and several visitors have asked about special orders." Malcolm's expression brightened as it always did when discussing books. "Mrs. Wong sold three of her art books, and young Simon from the pottery studio has been recommending craft guides to anyone who'll listen."

The mention of local success stories reminded me why we were doing this. The fair wasn't just about bringing literary culture to Tidehaven Cove, it was about supporting our local creative community and showing visitors what our village had to offer.

A commotion near the romance signing table drew my attention. Gary had apparently detoured from his path to the workshop and was now standing directly beside Colin's queue, addressing anyone who would listen.

"If you're interested in real literature," he was saying to a woman holding one of Colin's books, "you should consider political thrillers instead. They tackle actual issues rather than romantic fantasies designed to distract readers from genuine threats to democracy."

The woman looked confused and slightly offended, clutching her romance novel more tightly. Colin continued signing books with professional composure, but I could see tension in his shoulders. Both dogs had immediately focused on Gary again, their protective instincts reactivated.

"Excuse me," I said to Malcolm, already heading back across the green with my canine escorts trailing closely behind.

By the time I reached the signing table, Gary had launched into what appeared to be a full sales pitch. "My thriller 'Shadow of Power' exposes the kind of government corruption that threatens democracy itself. Publishers are too afraid to touch it because it reveals uncomfortable truths that challenge the establishment—"

"Mr. Stephens," I interrupted firmly, while Hardy positioned himself between Gary and the confused romance readers. "I believe you were heading to the research workshop?"

"Yes, but I thought these readers might benefit from exposure to more substantial literature—"

"I'm sure they appreciate the recommendation," I said, taking his arm and steering him away from the confused romance readers. "But the workshop starts in fifteen minutes, and I'd hate for you to miss it."

As I guided Gary away from Colin's table, I caught the romance writer's eye and mouthed "Sorry" over Gary's head. Colin nodded with a slight smile that suggested he was used to dealing with difficult personalities, though something in his expression seemed more strained than his usual professional composure.

"You know," Gary said as we walked, the dogs maintaining their protective formation around us, "that romance writer, Colin, is it? he's actually quite talented. With his understanding of character psychology, he could write something truly meaningful if he focused on real issues instead of manufactured emotional drama."

I found this assessment interesting, particularly since Gary had spent the last ten minutes dismissing romance as worthless propaganda. "Have you read his work?"

"Enough to recognize genuine skill being wasted on commercial manipulation," Gary replied with patronizing certainty. "His prose style shows real potential—it's just being applied to trivial subject matter instead of exposing actual threats to society."

We'd reached the village hall, where other workshop attendees were filing through the front entrance. I could see Diana Hartwell among them, looking perfectly composed despite Gary's earlier conspiracy theories about publishing suppression.

"I think you'll find this workshop very informative," I said, holding the door open while the dogs waited patiently beside me. "The leader has extensive experience with source verification."

"Good. Perhaps I can share some of my own authentication techniques—I've had to develop quite sophisticated methods for bypassing institutional censorship when researching governmental conspiracy." Gary straightened his shoulders, apparently preparing to dominate another literary discussion.

As he disappeared into the building, I allowed myself a moment of relief. The workshop would keep him occupied for at least an hour, giving the rest of us a peaceful interlude. Both dogs seemed to sense the temporary reprieve, with Hardy's tail finally resuming its normal cheerful wagging.

Walking back across the green, I noticed that Colin's signing line had doubled in length during Gary's interruption. Apparently controversy was good for business, even if it wasn't intended as marketing.

"How are we holding up?" Freya asked, appearing at my elbow with her usual spot-on timing. She was carrying a stack of Hampton Books tote bags and looked cheerfully harried. Both dogs immediately gravitated toward her, seeking reassurance after their morning of Gary surveillance.

"Surviving," I said. "Though I'm starting to understand why some literary events have security."

"Oh, people like Gary aren't so bad once you understand their pattern," Freya said confidently. "He's desperate for validation, so he tries to insert himself into every conversation about literature. Textbook insecurity masquerading as expertise."

"You sound like you've dealt with his type before."

"University is full of them, people who think being critical of popular success makes them intellectually superior." Freya grinned while giving Hardy an absent-minded pat. "The trick is giving them something to feel expert about. Watch this work on him later."

I had to admit, Freya's psychological insights were often surprisingly astute. Perhaps her academic background was more useful than I'd realized.

The morning continued with the usual fair dynamics, happy browsers, chattering children, and the pleasant buzz of a community event succeeding beyond expectations. Gary's absence during the workshop created a notably more relaxed atmosphere, though both dogs remained more alert than usual, as if they expected his disruptive presence to return at any moment.

By noon, when we broke for lunch, I was cautiously optimistic that we might actually pull off a successful literary festival. The afternoon would bring author readings, more workshops, and the evening social event, but so far everything was proceeding according to plan.

I should have known better than to tempt fate with such confidence.

As I headed toward the tea shop for a much-needed break, Malcolm appeared beside me, clearly bearing unwelcome news.

"Miss Hampton," he said quietly, "I think you should know. There's been rather a heated discussion in the historical research workshop. Something about proper attribution of sources and the ethics of collaborative research."

"Gary?" I asked, though I already knew the answer. Austen, who had been trotting beside me, immediately sat down and fixed her attention on Malcolm as if she too recognized the significance of this development.

"Indeed. He apparently accused another participant of using 'sanitized' sources instead of pursuing 'authentic' documentation. The workshop leader had to intervene before things became too unpleasant."

I closed my eyes briefly, already dreading the afternoon's possibilities. "What else?"

"He's signed up for Diana Hartwell's craft workshop this afternoon. And the 'meet the agent' session with Ms. Pemberton immediately after that."

Hardy had joined Austen in sitting attentively, both dogs apparently sensing that Gary's continued presence was going to mean more stress for their human.

The day was far from over, and Gary Stephens was just getting started.

"Right," I said with determined optimism, while both dogs looked up at me with expressions that clearly conveyed their doubt about this assessment. "How hard can one afternoon be?"

3

———

The afternoon session of Diana Hartwell's craft workshop was held in the cleared back room of Hampton Books, surrounded by towering shelves of mysteries and thrillers that seemed to watch over the proceedings with literary authority. Fifteen aspiring writers had crowded into the space, notebooks ready and faces bright with the hope of unlocking professional secrets.

I'd positioned myself near the doorway with Austen and Hardy settled at my feet, ostensibly to handle any logistical issues but actually to monitor Gary's behavior. So far, he'd been surprisingly well-behaved, taking detailed notes as Diana discussed the importance of pacing in thriller narratives.

"The key to maintaining tension," Diana was saying, "is knowing when to reveal information and when to withhold it. Readers need to feel they're always on the verge of understanding something crucial."

A woman in her sixties raised her hand. "But how do you know if you're revealing too much too early?"

"Excellent question, Mrs. Lupin. The answer is usually

found in your beta readers' responses. If they're guessing your major plot twist by chapter three, you've shown your hand too soon."

Gary's hand shot up immediately. "That assumes your readers want predictable entertainment," he said without waiting to be called upon. "What about literature that challenges people to think beyond comfortable patterns? Political fiction needs to shake readers out of complacency, not follow formulaic structures."

The room fell into uncomfortable silence. Diana's professional smile didn't waver, but I could see her shoulders stiffen slightly. Hardy lifted his head from his paws, ears pricked toward Gary with renewed attention.

"You raise an interesting point about different genres having different goals," Diana replied diplomatically. "Though I'd argue that even challenging literature benefits from solid storytelling fundamentals."

"But surely you'd agree that political thrillers operate under different rules entirely?" Gary leaned forward in his chair, clearly warming to his theme. "When you're exposing real duplicity, artificial plot devices actually weaken the impact."

Remembering Freya's advice about giving Gary something to feel expert about, I decided to try her technique.

"Mr. Stephens," I interjected gently, "it sounds like you've given a lot of thought to the unique challenges of political fiction. What specific techniques have you found most effective for maintaining authenticity?"

Gary's entire demeanor shifted, his defensive posture relaxing as he seized the opportunity to share his expertise. "Well, the most important thing is refusing to compromise for dramatic convenience. My political thriller, for instance, exposes actual governmental conspiracy—not invented conflict designed to create artificial tension."

"That must require extensive research," I continued, watching Diana's grateful expression as Gary's attention moved away from challenging her workshop structure.

"Exactly! Real investigative work, not the sanitized research that most thriller writers rely on. I've uncovered patterns of institutional corruption that go back decades, connections between powerful interests that they don't want exposed in popular literature."

A younger man near the back spoke up. "But how do you verify that kind of information? How do you know your sources are reliable?"

"You develop instincts for truth," Gary replied with evangelical fervor. "When you're dealing with systematic suppression of information, you can't trust conventional verification methods. The establishment controls those channels."

Diana seized the opportunity to redirect the conversation. "That's certainly one approach to research. Though most publishers do require verifiable sources for claims about real people and institutions..."

"Publishers!" Gary's voice rose with familiar passion. "Publishers are part of the problem! They demand 'verification' from the same institutions they're protecting. It's circular logic designed to suppress uncomfortable revelations."

I could see the other workshop participants beginning to look uncomfortable as Gary's conspiracy theories dominated what was supposed to be a craft discussion. Austen had risen to a sitting position, her alert posture suggesting she was picking up on the tension in the room.

"Perhaps," Diana suggested with admirable patience,

"we could discuss how different authors handle controversial subject matter? Mrs. Victor, didn't you mention that your domestic fiction often addresses social issues?"

Angela Victor, the middle-aged woman who had been taking copious notes, looked up eagerly. "Oh yes, I think literature has a responsibility to illuminate the problems in everyday life, family dynamics, community pressures, the small betrayals that happen between ordinary people."

"Small betrayals," Gary repeated with obvious disdain. "While the country faces institutional conspiracy that threatens democracy itself, we're worried about hurt feelings in suburban marriages?"

Angela's face flushed. "We're writing fiction, for goodness sake, not hard-hitting news articles! Literature doesn't have to solve world problems to have value."

"Excuse me, but domestic relationships are the foundation of society. If you can't write authentically about how people actually interact, what makes you think you can tackle larger political issues?"

"Because larger political issues matter more than whether someone's husband remembered their anniversary," Gary shot back. "Literature should prepare readers for real threats, not comfort them with familiar emotional patterns."

"Real threats like what?" Angela demanded, her voice rising. "Government conspiracies that exist only in paranoid fantasies? At least my characters behave like actual human beings instead of political mouthpieces!"

The workshop was rapidly deteriorating into exactly the kind of genre warfare that could poison the entire fair's atmosphere. Diana was making valiant attempts to restore order, but Gary and Angela were too focused on their mutual antagonism to listen.

"My characters expose truths that comfortable domestic fiction ignores," Gary declared. "They're willing to sacrifice personal happiness to protect democracy from corruption that people like your characters would never even notice."

"Your characters probably don't sound like real people at all," Angela retorted. "They probably deliver political speeches instead of having actual conversations!"

I could see that my attempt at Freya's technique had backfired spectacularly. Instead of giving Gary a constructive outlet for his expertise, I'd accidentally provided him with a platform to alienate another workshop participant.

"Perhaps," I interjected smoothly, "we could return to Diana's original discussion of pacing techniques? I'm sure there are methods that work across all genres."

"Actually," Diana said with diplomatic grace, "this discussion highlights an important point about knowing your audience. Different readers come to books seeking different experiences, and successful authors understand how to deliver what their specific audience wants."

"But what if what audiences want isn't what they need?" Gary pressed. "What if commercial success requires avoiding the very truths that literature should be revealing?"

"Then you write the books you believe need to be written," Diana replied simply. "But you also accept that the audience for challenging work might be smaller than the audience for entertaining work."

Gary's expression suggested he found this advice fundamentally unsatisfying, but before he could voice his objections, the workshop time was up and participants began gathering their materials.

"Ms. Hartwell," Gary called as Diana prepared to leave, "I wonder if I could ask your opinion about a specific scene in my manuscript? You might find my approach to revealing official corruption quite innovative."

Diana's smile was polite but firm. "I'm afraid I don't have time for individual manuscript consultations this weekend. Perhaps you could submit through proper channels?"

"Proper channels," Gary muttered as Diana escaped. "More gatekeeping designed to prevent challenging work from reaching readers."

After the workshop participants dispersed, I found myself helping to restack chairs while Angela Victor lingered near the front of the room, still visibly agitated from her argument with Gary.

"That man is insufferable," she said without preamble. "I've met plenty of difficult writers, but his arrogance is extraordinary. Someone should teach him that dismissing other people's work doesn't make his own work more important."

"He does seem very... passionate about his theories," I replied diplomatically.

"Passionate? He's delusional!" Angela's face was still flushed with anger. "Writers like him give literature a bad name. Maybe if someone explained some basic manners to him, he'd learn to participate in discussions without insulting everyone else's genres."

As Angela stormed off toward the tea shop, presumably to calm down with a restorative cup of Earl Grey, I couldn't help thinking that Gary's ability to alienate people was truly impressive in its efficiency.

"Well," I said to Austen and Hardy, who had remained remarkably patient during the literary warfare, "Freya's technique needs some refinement."

4

The evening social event was winding down when I spotted the familiar figure emerging from a taxi near the village green. Even in the gathering dusk, Beauregard Morrison's perfectly tailored traveling clothes and confident stride were unmistakable. He hefted a leather carry-on bag from the taxi's boot, then turned to survey the scene with obvious appreciation.

My heart did a little skip. Part pleasure at seeing an old friend, part apprehension at how his arrival might complicate the already tense atmosphere of the fair.

"Ginny!" His warm Southern accent carried across the green as he approached with a genuine smile. "My word, this place is even more charming than your emails suggested."

I found myself grinning despite my exhaustion. "Beau! You're early. I thought you weren't arriving until tomorrow."

"Changed my flight when I realized I might miss most of the fair." He enveloped me in one of his signature hugs, the kind that reminded you why people fell for Southern charm. "Though from the looks of things, I may have timed this perfectly. That gentleman over there appears to be having quite the animated discussion with thin air."

Following his gaze, I saw Gary pacing near the information booth, gesticulating wildly while clutching his manila folder. Most of the evening's attendees had given him a wide berth, creating an invisible circle of social isolation around his increasingly agitated monologue.

"And these must be the famous literary assistants," Beau said, crouching down to properly greet both dogs. "I've missed you two."

"That's right. They've been keeping watch over the fair's more challenging participants." I gestured toward Gary's solitary performance. "That's Gary Stephens, our resident literary gadfly. He's managed to alienate every publishing professional at the fair in the span of one afternoon."

"Impressive efficiency." Beau studied Gary with the professional interest I remembered from our Charleston days. "What's his particular brand of delusion?"

"Political thriller writer convinced that his manuscript exposes government corruption too dangerous for publishers to touch. He's spent the day explaining to anyone who'll listen why the entire industry is part of a vast conspiracy against truth-telling."

Beau's eyebrows rose slightly. "Ah. The paranoid genius variety. I've met the type."

I felt a surge of gratitude for his understanding. "I have to admit, I feel lucky I've never encountered this level of... intensity before. In corporate publishing, we mostly dealt with professional authors and agents. This is new territory for me."

"Count yourself fortunate. Literary festivals attract them like magnets. Authors convinced their lack of success proves a grand conspiracy rather than, say, an unmarketable manuscript." His tone was affectionately cynical. "Though I must say, most don't take their case to quite such public forums."

As if summoned by our conversation, Gary suddenly pivoted in our direction and began striding toward us with obvious purpose. I suppressed a groan while both dogs immediately moved closer to me, their relaxed greeting behavior shifting back to protective alertness.

"Miss Hampton!" he called while still several yards away. "I need to discuss the evening's programming. There's been a serious oversight in the representation of serious literature."

"Mr. Stephens, this is my friend Beauregard Morrison from Charleston. Beau, Gary Stephens."

Beau extended his hand with polished Southern courtesy. "Pleasure to meet you, Mr. Stephens. I understand you're a writer?"

"Political thriller specialist," Gary replied, his handshake perfunctory as his attention remained fixed on me. "Miss Hampton, I've reviewed tonight's reading selections, and I notice they're all genre fiction—romance, cozy mysteries, historical sagas. Where's the representation for literature that tackles real-world issues?"

"The readers volunteered to share their favorite published works for tonight's late readings," I explained diplomatically. "It wasn't curated by genre."

"But that's exactly the problem!" Gary's voice rose enough to draw glances from nearby fairgoers. "When left to choose freely, people gravitate toward escapist entertainment instead of confronting uncomfortable realities. That's why the publishing industry has abandoned its responsibility to educate readers about actual threats to democracy."

Beau's expression remained pleasantly neutral, but I

caught the slight tightening around his eyes that indicated professional wariness. "That's an interesting perspective, Mr. Stephens. Do you find that political themes require different narrative approaches than other genres?"

"Absolutely!" Gary seized on Beau's comment with obvious relief at finding apparent engagement. "Entertainment fiction can indulge in artificial conflicts and convenient resolutions, but political thrillers must grapple with systemic corruption that can't be solved by individual heroics. My manuscript 'Shadow of Power' exposes governmental malfeasance that goes right to the constitutional level."

"Publishing can certainly be challenging for authors tackling controversial subjects," Beau agreed diplomatically. "Are you working with an agent currently?"

"I was, but she dropped me when publishers started pressuring agencies to avoid politically sensitive material." Gary pulled his folder closer to his chest. "The deeper you dig into real conspiracy, the more resistance you encounter from people who benefit from the status quo."

I exchanged a quick glance with Beau, whose diplomatic smile was becoming slightly strained.

"Between positions myself at the moment," Beau said smoothly. "Left my previous agency and decided on a sabbatical before diving into anything new. Always interested in compelling work, though market fit is obviously crucial."

"Market fit," Gary repeated with obvious disdain. "Code words for 'safe enough not to threaten anyone powerful.' But surely someone with your background understands that some truths transcend commercial considerations?"

I noticed Colin Mitchell glancing over from where he was signing the last few books of the evening. His expression was carefully neutral, but something in his posture suggested he was listening to our conversation with unusual attention.

"Truth is certainly valuable," Beau said carefully. "Though fiction's relationship to reality can be complex—"

"There's nothing complex about corruption and conspiracy," Gary interrupted. "Either you expose it or you participate in covering it up. Most publishers have chosen the latter because it's financially safer than confronting powerful interests."

The conversation was attracting more attention than I was comfortable with. Several other authors had paused their own discussions to observe Gary's increasingly animated lecture.

"Mr. Stephens," I interjected gently, "perhaps we could continue this discussion tomorrow? I'm sure Beau would love to hear more about your work after he's had a chance to get settled."

"Of course, of course." Gary seemed to realize he'd been monopolizing the conversation. "But I hope you'll consider adding some balance to tomorrow's programming. There are people here who need to understand that literature can serve purposes beyond mere entertainment—that it can expose the kind of institutional corruption that threatens the very foundation of democratic society."

After Gary wandered off toward the tea shop, presumably to corner other unsuspecting fairgoers, Beau turned to me with raised eyebrows.

"Well," he said mildly. "That was illuminating."

"I'm sorry about that. He's been like this all day."

"No need to apologize. I've encountered worse at industry conferences." Beau's expression grew thoughtful. "Though I have to say, there's something familiar about his manuscript description. Political thriller, government corruption, institutional conspiracies. I feel like I've heard that pitch before."

"Really? Where?"

"Can't quite place it. Probably just the standard themes that conspiracy thriller writers tend to gravitate toward." He shrugged. "They all start to sound alike after a while, shadow governments, judicial corruption, constitutional crises. The paranoid political subgenre has very predictable patterns."

Hardy had settled at my feet again, while Austen continued to monitor Gary's progress toward the tea shop with watchful eyes.

"Actually," Beau said, his voice taking on a more serious tone, "watching Gary's behavior reminds me of something I've been investigating in my consulting work. There's been an uptick in amateur writers claiming to have uncovered real conspiracies that publishers are suppressing. Most of it's harmless delusion, but occasionally these cases involve more serious underlying issues."

"What kind of issues?" I asked.

"Identity theft, plagiarism, fraudulent submissions, people so desperate to be published that they'll claim any work as their own if they think it might succeed." Beau glanced back toward Gary, who was now holding court near Elspeth's tea shop. "Gary's defensive behavior and his elaborate theories about suppression could indicate he's hiding something about the authenticity of his manuscript."

Before I could respond, we were interrupted by Malcolm appearing at my elbow with his usual impeccable timing.

"Miss Hampton, Mr. Morrison, I presume? Welcome to Tidehaven Cove." Malcolm's formal greeting was accompanied by a slight bow that managed to be both respectful and slightly theatrical.

"Thank you," Beau replied. "I hope my early arrival isn't creating additional complications during such a busy weekend."

"Not at all. You are staying with Ms. Hampton so I'm not involved in preparations."

I tried not to shudder at the thought of Malcolm sorting through my linens and preparing my guest room.

As Malcolm departed to oversee the evening's cleanup, Beau turned back to me with a look I remembered from our Charleston days, sharp and questioning.

"So," he said quietly, "what aren't you telling me about Mr. Stephens? Because that wasn't just garden-variety author desperation I witnessed."

I glanced around to make sure we weren't being overheard. "He's been increasingly hostile as the day went on. Started with interrupting children's story time to critique the educational value of fantasy, escalated to public confrontations with agents and workshop participants. By this evening, he was practically radioactive. No one wanted to be near him."

"And tomorrow he'll still be here, presumably even more frustrated after a night to stew over his grievances."

"Exactly." I felt a knot of worry tighten in my stomach. "Beau, I'm starting to think having him at this fair was a mistake. He bought his own ticket, so it wasn't like I could have screened him out, but he's not just difficult; he's becoming genuinely disruptive."

"These situations usually resolve themselves," Beau said reassuringly. "Most authors like Gary eventually exhaust themselves with their own drama and either calm down or remove themselves from the situation."

"I hope you're right."

As the evening's attendees began making their way toward the late-night readings, I caught sight of Dr. Harrington emerging from the village hall where he'd been helping with cleanup. His usually calm demeanor seemed slightly strained as his gaze found me across the green.

"Ginny," he called, approaching with his characteristic measured stride. "Everything sorted for the evening?"

"Just about. Elliot, I'd like you to meet my friend Beauregard Morrison from Charleston. Beau, Dr. Elliot Harrington, our local veterinarian."

The two men shook hands with polite civility, but I couldn't miss the subtle tension in the exchange. Elliot's grip lasted a fraction longer than necessary, while Beau's smile carried just a hint of Southern charm that could be interpreted as either friendliness or mild challenge.

"Pleasure to meet you, Doctor," Beau said warmly. "Ginny's mentioned you in her letters. Thank you for looking after her during her transition to village life."

"It's been my pleasure," Elliot replied, his tone carefully neutral. "I understand you're visiting for the fair?"

"A long-overdue vacation, actually. Though I suspect I'll end up helping with literary emergencies anyway—old habits die hard." Beau's laugh was easy and confident. "Between positions at the moment, so the timing worked out perfectly for a proper English countryside experience."

"I'm sure your expertise will be valuable," Elliot said. "Though I imagine Ginny has everything well organized."

The conversation continued for several more minutes with perfect politeness that somehow managed to feel like a very civilized territorial dispute. I found myself caught between amusement and exasperation at the obvious masculine posturing disguised as literary small talk.

"Right," I said finally, "I should get Beau settled at the cottage. Early start tomorrow with the morning workshops."

"Of course," Elliot agreed. "I'll see you tomorrow, then. Both of you."

As we walked toward the cottage with the dogs trotting alongside us, Beau was oddly quiet. Finally, he spoke with carefully casual tone.

"Nice fellow, the good doctor. Very... protective."

"Elliot's been a good friend," I replied, perhaps a bit more defensively than necessary.

"I'm sure he has. Intuition tells me there might be more than friendship involved, but I could be wrong." His tone was light, but something underneath suggested the observation mattered to him.

5

S aturday morning dawned crisp and clear, a perfect autumn day that made browsing outdoor book stalls seem absolutely essential. I stood at my cottage window with my first cup of coffee, watching early fairgoers already making their way across the green. Both Austen and Hardy sat beside me, alert and ready for another day of literary supervision.

"Beautiful morning," Beau observed, emerging from the guest room fully dressed despite the early hour. His ability to look perfectly put-together at seven AM had always impressed and slightly annoyed me.

"It is. Though I'm hoping it stays peaceful longer than yesterday did."

Through the window, I could see Gary's white Ford already parked near the village hall. My heart sank at the sight, apparently he was planning another full day of literary evangelism.

"Coffee?" I offered, gesturing toward the kitchen.

"Please. And then you can brief me on today's danger zones." Beau's tone was light, but I caught the underlying concern. He'd been doing this longer than I had and recognized the signs of an event spiraling toward crisis.

As I prepared his coffee, both dogs suddenly perked up at the sound of voices outside. Through the kitchen window, I could see early fairgoers already making their way down Cottage Lane toward the green.

"We should probably head over soon," I said, handing Beau his cup. "Get there before—"

A raised voice carried from the direction of the village center, though the words were indistinct from this distance.

"Oh no," I muttered. "That sounds like it might be Gary already."

"Starting early, is he?" Beau joined me at the window, though we could only see the lane and part of the green from here. "Should we investigate?"

"Definitely. Let me just grab my jacket."

"That man has a talent for making enemies," Beau observed. "What's the history between him and the antiques dealer?"

"Oliver hosted Gary's workshop yesterday in his back room. Apparently Gary spent most of it explaining how historical authentication is used to suppress evidence of governmental conspiracy." I handed Beau his coffee, while the dogs maintained their vigil at the window. "Oliver takes authenticity very seriously. It's his professional livelihood. Gary's theories about 'manufactured legitimacy' probably felt like a personal attack."

"Understandable. Most dealers I've met would have physically ejected someone questioning their authentication methods." Beau sipped his coffee thoughtfully. "Though Oliver agreed to host the workshop, so presumably he's more tolerant than most."

"Or more desperate for the rental income," I said. "Oliver's been trying to buy the bookshop for his expansion. Hosting workshop space probably seemed like easy money."

A knock at the front door interrupted our surveillance. Both dogs immediately abandoned the window to investigate this new development, their tails wagging as familiar voices carried through the door.

"That'll be Malcolm and Freya," I said, opening the door to find my two employees looking unusually serious for such an early hour.

"Good morning, Miss Hampton," Malcolm said formally, though his eyes immediately found Beau with curious interest. "I hope we're not intruding, but there's been a development."

"What kind of development?" I asked, stepping aside to let them in while the dogs performed their morning greeting ritual.

"Gary cornered Marcus Webb in the pub last night," Freya announced without preamble. "Apparently it got quite heated before the landlord intervened."

"Define heated," Beau said, though his attention remained on Malcolm. "And good morning, Malcolm."

"Good morning, Mr. Morrison," Malcolm replied with a slight nod. "By heated, I mean Gary accused Mr. Webb of deliberately publishing 'safe' authors while suppressing politically dangerous material." His tone carried the carefully controlled outrage of someone reporting scandalous behavior. "He then proceeded to explain exactly why Moorland Press was contributing to the intellectual impoverishment of British readers."

"In front of the entire pub," Freya added helpfully. "Including several other authors and at least three local reviewers."

I felt my stomach drop. Marcus Webb ran one of the few

remaining independent presses specializing in literary fiction and quality thrillers. His reputation was built on discovering overlooked talent and taking risks on unconventional narratives, exactly the opposite of the 'safe commercial publishing' Gary claimed to oppose.

"How did Marcus respond?" I asked, though I suspected I didn't want to know.

"Initially tried to engage professionally," Malcolm replied. "Explained his editorial philosophy, mentioned several controversial books he'd published despite commercial risk. But Gary dismissed everything as 'controlled opposition designed to create the illusion of brave publishing while avoiding real threats to institutional power.'"

"Good lord," I muttered, while both dogs sensed my stress and moved closer to my legs. "What happened then?"

"Marcus lost his temper," Freya said with obvious relish for the drama. "Told Gary that if he wanted to see real conspiracy, he should look at authors who blame publishing houses for their own lack of talent. Said maybe the problem wasn't institutional suppression but basic writing quality."

Beau whistled softly. "That must have gone over well."

"Gary started shouting about elitist gatekeeping and academic bias," Malcolm continued. "Claimed that criticism of his manuscript proved Marcus was part of the establishment conspiracy. The landlord had to threaten to call Constable Trewin before Gary finally left."

"And Marcus?" I asked.

"Stayed for several more pints, according to Elspeth," Freya reported. "She said he was muttering something about 'delusional amateurs' and 'time-wasting parasites on real literature.'"

This was what I'd been dreading. Gary's conspiracy theories weren't just annoying people anymore, they were creating real professional conflicts between people who needed to work together. The literary community was small enough that these kinds of feuds could have lasting consequences.

"Right," I said with determined optimism that fooled no one, least of all the dogs. "Let's get to the fair and try some damage control."

"Actually," Beau said thoughtfully, "I'd like to observe Gary's behavior before intervening. His escalating hostility suggests he's working toward something, either a complete breakdown or a final confrontation. Understanding his pattern might help us manage whatever comes next."

As we walked across the green toward the already-bustling fair, I noticed several conversations that stopped abruptly when we approached. News of the pub incident had clearly spread through the village grapevine with characteristic efficiency.

"There's our literary terrorist," Freya murmured, nodding toward the village hall where Gary was setting up what appeared to be an impromptu information booth. He'd arranged a folding table with stacks of papers and a hand-lettered sign reading "TRUTH IN LITERATURE: Exposing Publishing Conspiracy."

"Oh good," I said weakly. "He's decided to make it official."

Marcus Webb was visible near the poetry corner, looking distinctly haggard despite his rumpled attempt at professional appearance. His normally cheerful demeanor had been replaced by obvious irritation as he arranged books with sharp, angry movements.

"I should probably apologize to Marcus," I said. "This is supposed to be a relaxing weekend for our visiting professionals, not a battleground."

"Let me handle that," Beau suggested. "Publisher to publisher, as it were. You focus on keeping Gary contained."

As Beau headed toward Marcus, I approached Gary's self-appointed truth-telling station with Malcolm and Freya flanking me like diplomatic bodyguards. Both dogs immediately shifted into their protective formation, positioning themselves between Gary and me.

"Mr. Stephens," I said with forced cheerfulness, "I see you're expanding your participation in the fair."

"Miss Hampton! Perfect timing." Gary's eyes gleamed with evangelical fervor. "I've prepared informational materials about the systematic suppression of political literature. People need to understand what they're not being allowed to read."

The papers on his table appeared to be photocopied excerpts from various conspiracy websites, annotated with Gary's handwritten commentary about publishing industry corruption. Several early fairgoers had paused to examine his display with expressions ranging from puzzlement to alarm.

"That's very... thorough of you," I managed. "Though I should mention that our insurance requires vendor tables to be officially registered with the event coordination."

"Vendor table?" Gary's voice rose with indignation. "This isn't commerce, it's education! I'm providing essential information about the threats to literary freedom that commercial interests want to suppress!"

"Perhaps we could find you space in the information tent?" Malcolm said. "Less wind exposure for your materials, and easier access for interested readers."

"The information tent is controlled by the same commercial interests that organize this entire fair," Gary replied suspiciously. "How do I know my materials won't be censored or suppressed?"

"Because," Freya said with sweet reasonableness, "it's a village book fair, not the Pentagon. The most controversial decision we've made is whether to serve Earl Grey or English Breakfast at the tea stand."

Her attempt at humor was lost on Gary, whose paranoia was clearly beyond the reach of gentle mockery. He clutched his papers closer to his chest as if protecting them from imminent confiscation.

"You may think this is amusing," he said with wounded dignity, "but there are people at this fair who need to understand that literature can serve higher purposes than entertainment. My materials expose connections between publishing houses and governmental interests that most people never even suspect exist."

A middle-aged woman browsing nearby paused to examine one of Gary's photocopied articles. "Is this about those American conspiracy theories?" she asked with polite curiosity. "The ones about the deep state and global cabals?"

"This is about documented corruption that transcends national boundaries," Gary replied earnestly. "Publishing houses worldwide collaborate to suppress political fiction that exposes institutional malfeasance. My research reveals patterns of—"

"Right," the woman said, backing away with obvious alarm. "Well. Good luck with that."

As she hurried toward the safer territory of the romance stall, I noticed Oliver Blackthorn emerging from his shop and surveying Gary's unauthorized information station with obvious displeasure.

"Problem?" Oliver asked curtly, approaching our little group with quick, angry steps.

"No problem," I said quickly. "Just discussing logistics."

"Because unauthorized vendors violate village regulations," Oliver continued, his gaze fixed on Gary's improvised table. "Commercial activities require proper permits and insurance documentation."

"This isn't commercial," Gary protested. "It's educational—"

"It's disruption," Oliver interrupted sharply. "Same as yesterday's workshop disruption and last night's pub disruption. Some of us are trying to run legitimate businesses without amateur conspiracy theorists poisoning the atmosphere."

The confrontation was attracting more attention than I could handle diplomatically. Several other authors had paused their own activities to observe the developing conflict, while fairgoers began giving our area a wide berth.

"Perhaps," Malcolm suggested with admirable calm, "we could relocate this discussion to a less central location?"

Gary was beyond diplomatic management now, his defensive anger finally finding a target in Oliver's obvious hostility.

"Legitimate business?" Gary's voice carried clearly across the green. "You sell overpriced antiques to tourists while lecturing everyone about authenticity! At least my work exposes real corruption instead of manufacturing artificial value for decorative objects!"

"My antiques have documented provenance and verified authenticity," Oliver shot back. "They don't rely on paranoid fantasies and internet conspiracy theories!"

"Documented by whom? The same institutional authorities that control publishing, museums, and academic research?" Gary was fully engaged now, his papers forgotten as he faced Oliver with obvious relish for the confrontation.

"Your 'authentication' process is exactly the kind of gate-keeping that suppresses uncomfortable historical realities!"

Both dogs had moved closer to me, their earlier alertness shifting to genuine concern as the argument escalated. Neither of them barked, but I heard a low rumble in Austen's throat, and Hardy stood like a linebacker ready to block a play.

"Mr. Stephens," I interjected firmly, "I think we should—"

"No," Oliver said coldly, "let him finish. I'd like to hear exactly how historical authentication constitutes conspiracy. It might explain why his 'political thriller' reads like amateur paranoia instead of serious literature."

"You've read my manuscript?" Gary demanded, his voice cracking with surprise and indignation.

"Enough to recognize derivative garbage when I see it," Oliver replied with cutting precision. "Bad writing is bad writing, regardless of the author's political theories."

The public nature of this humiliation was clearly more than Gary could tolerate. His face flushed with anger and embarrassment as other fairgoers began to slow down and openly stare at the escalating confrontation.

"You have no right to judge work you don't understand," he said, his voice shaking with rage. "You're just an antiques dealer who profits from fake authenticity! What would you know about real literature that exposes actual truth instead of selling pretty lies to tourists?"

"People like me," Oliver said with icy calm, "recognize quality when we see it. And we're not impressed by conspiracy theories masquerading as literature."

I could see the situation was completely out of hand, but before I could attempt another intervention, Beau appeared at my elbow with Marcus Webb in tow.

"Gentlemen," Beau said with smooth authority, "perhaps we could continue this fascinating discussion of authenticity and authority over coffee? I'd be very interested in both your perspectives on the relationship between commercial and artistic value."

His intervention had the desired effect of breaking the immediate confrontation, though Gary's fury was clearly barely controlled. Oliver stepped back with obvious reluctance, apparently recognizing that the public argument was no longer serving his interests.

"Fine," Gary said, gathering his materials with shaking hands. "But this conversation isn't over. There are people at this fair who deserve to know how the literary establishment really operates."

As Gary stalked away toward the tea shop, presumably to find a more sympathetic audience for his theories, Oliver turned to me with an expression that managed to combine apology and irritation.

"Sorry about that, Ginny. But that man's been a disruption since yesterday morning, and someone needed to address his behavior directly."

"I understand your frustration," I replied diplomatically. "Though perhaps next time we could handle these conflicts a bit more privately?"

"Next time," Oliver said with grim determination, "I certainly hope there won't be a next time. People like Gary Stephens poison community events for everyone else. The sooner he removes himself from this fair, the better for all of us."

As Oliver returned to his shop, Marcus Webb shook his head with obvious disgust.

"I've dealt with difficult authors before," he said to Beau, "but that level of delusion is genuinely unsettling. He's convinced himself that any criticism of his work proves a vast conspiracy against him personally."

"Unfortunately common in my experience," Beau replied sympathetically. "Authors who can't tell the difference between editorial feedback and personal persecution tend to create these kinds of public scenes."

6

_____

The afternoon workshops were scheduled to begin at two o'clock, which gave me just enough time to grab a quick sandwich from Elspeth's tea shop and check that all the room assignments were properly sorted. Gary had mercifully abandoned his conspiracy booth around noon, though not before distributing his photocopied materials to anyone unfortunate enough to make eye contact with him.

"Where did he go?" I asked Malcolm as we did a final sweep of the preparations.

"Last seen heading toward Oliver's workshop," Malcolm replied grimly. "The 'Advanced Manuscript Critique' session starts in ten minutes."

I felt my stomach clench. Gary attending a manuscript critique workshop was asking for trouble. "Should I go check on them?"

"Give it a few minutes," Freya suggested, appearing with a stack of feedback forms. "Maybe Angela can handle him better in a smaller group setting."

Both dogs had been unusually restless all afternoon,

following me more closely than usual and occasionally stopping to stare toward Oliver's shop with worried expressions. Hardy kept making small whining sounds, while Austen sat rigid and watchful.

"The dogs seem on edge," Beau observed, crouching down to give Hardy a reassuring pat. "Think they're picking up on all the tension from this morning?"

"Probably. They've been Gary's unofficial early warning system since he arrived." I glanced at my watch. "The workshop should be starting now. Think I should—"

A sharp sound carried from Oliver's shop—something between a crash and a bang, followed by raised voices.

Both dogs immediately perked up, their ears swiveling toward the sound like radar. Hardy took a step in that direction, then looked back at me as if asking permission to investigate.

"That doesn't sound good," Freya muttered.

"I should go check," I said, already moving toward Oliver's shop with the dogs trotting beside me. "Maybe I can defuse whatever's happening before it gets out of hand."

"We'll come with you," Beau said, falling into step alongside Malcolm and Freya.

Oliver's antique shop occupied a narrow Victorian building wedged between the post office and a small art gallery. The front windows displayed carefully arranged period furniture and decorative objects, while a discrete sign indicated that workshops were held in the "consultation room" at the rear of the building.

As we approached, I could hear voices through the partially open front door. Someone was speaking with barely controlled frustration: "—completely inappropriate venue for that kind of discussion. This is a craft workshop, not a political debate forum."

"But surely authenticity in writing requires the same principles as authenticity in antiques?" Gary's voice was equally heated. "If the antiques business can't face uncomfortable truths about gatekeeping and manufactured legitimacy, how can writers be expected to expose similar corruption in literature?"

"Mr. Stephens," another voice interjected, Angela Victor, who was leading the session. "Perhaps we could focus on the actual craft elements we're here to discuss?"

"The craft elements are exactly what I'm addressing," Gary replied with condescending patience. "Political fiction requires different techniques because it serves different purposes than escapist entertainment."

I exchanged glances with Beau, both of us recognizing the familiar pattern of Gary's escalating rhetoric. Through the shop window, I could see several workshop participants looking increasingly uncomfortable as the discussion devolved into Gary's standard conspiracy lecture.

"This was predictable," Malcolm murmured. "Mr. Stephens appears constitutionally incapable of participating in literary discussions without inserting his theories about suppression in a respectable industry."

Both dogs had stopped just outside the shop entrance. Hardy's tail had dropped to half-mast, while Austen was doing her statue impression, waiting to spring into action.

"I'm going in," I decided. "Before this gets completely out of hand."

The interior of Oliver's shop was a maze of carefully arranged antique furniture, with narrow pathways between display areas leading toward the back room where workshops were held. The sound of raised voices was much clearer from inside, though the words were still partially muffled by the closed consultation room door.

"—refuse to engage with the actual issues because you're invested in maintaining the status quo that benefits established interests," Gary was saying as I approached the rear of the shop.

"I'm invested in helping writers improve their craft," Angela's voice replied, strained with obvious effort at maintaining professional composure. "Not in entertaining paranoid political theories."

I knocked gently on the consultation room door. "Everything all right in here?"

"Ginny, perfect timing," Angela said, opening the door with visible relief. Oliver appeared behind her, looking grateful for the interruption. "We were just discussing the difference between constructive criticism and conspiracy theories."

The consultation room was cramped but comfortable, with six chairs arranged around a small table covered in manuscript pages and notebooks. Four of the six participants remained seated, looking various degrees of uncomfortable, while Gary stood near the window with his arms crossed defensively.

"Mr. Stephens was explaining his theories about how editorial feedback is designed to suppress political content," Angela said with acid sweetness. "Apparently my suggestion that his protagonist needs more character development proves I'm part of the literary establishment conspiracy."

"Character development is a distraction technique," Gary replied earnestly. "When you're exposing real rot at the core of the government, artificial personality conflicts weaken the impact of the harsh reality. Readers need to focus on the institutional malfeasance, not invented emotional drama."

"Perhaps," I suggested diplomatically, "we could take a short break? Give everyone a chance to—"

"I don't need a break," Gary interrupted. "I need people to understand that political fiction operates under different rules than commercial entertainment. My manuscript exposes actual corruption—it can't be evaluated using the same standards as fantasy novels or romance stories."

"Your manuscript," Angela said with cutting precision, "can't be evaluated at all because it reads like a paranoid manifesto rather than coherent fiction."

The room fell into uncomfortable silence. Gary's face flushed with humiliation and rage, while the other workshop participants looked like they wanted to disappear into their chairs.

"That's enough," I said firmly. "Mr. Stephens, perhaps we could discuss your manuscript privately? I'd be happy to arrange a separate consultation—"

"I'm tired of being silenced by people who benefit from maintaining ignorant populations," Gary said, his voice shaking. "Everyone in this room needs to understand how the literary establishment really operates."

He pulled his familiar manila folder from his bag and began extracting pages. "My manuscript 'Shadow of Power' exposes connections between publishing houses and governmental interests that go right to the constitutional level. The reason it's being rejected isn't quality. It's because the truth threatens powerful people."

"Mr. Stephens," Angela said with strained patience, "this is neither the time nor the place for political lectures. We're here to discuss writing craft, not conspiracy theories."

"Writing craft?" Gary's voice rose to near-shouting. "You mean the artificial techniques designed to make challenging literature palatable to establishment interests? The structural formulas that neuter political content to make it safe for commercial publication?"

I could see the situation was completely out of hand. The other workshop participants were gathering their materials with obvious intention to leave, while Oliver's expression had shifted from professional irritation to genuine anger.

"I think we should end the workshop here," I announced. "Thank you all for participating, and we'll see you at this evening's—"

"People need to hear this," Gary said desperately. "The systematic suppression of political literature affects every writer in this room, whether they realize it or not."

But the other participants were already filing out, murmuring polite excuses while clearly eager to escape the increasingly uncomfortable atmosphere. Within moments, only Gary, Angela, Oliver, and I remained in the consultation room, along with the tension that seemed to fill the small space.

"Mr. Stephens," Angela said firmly, "I'm going to ask you to leave. Your behavior is disruptive and inappropriate for a literary event."

Oliver nodded his agreement from where he stood near the door. "My shop, my rules. You need to go."

"You can't silence truth by ejecting the messenger," Gary replied, but his voice had lost some of its earlier conviction. Being abandoned by his audience had clearly shaken his confidence.

"I can eject disruptive individuals from my workshop," Angela countered. "Which is what you are."

I could see Gary struggling between his desire to continue his lecture and his recognition that his audience had fled. Finally, he gathered his papers with shaking hands.

"This proves exactly what I've been saying," he muttered. "The moment someone tries to expose uncomfortable realities, the establishment closes ranks to silence them."

As Gary headed toward the shop's front entrance, both dogs immediately moved to flank me, their protective instincts clearly activated by the lingering tension in the room.

"I'm sorry about that," I said to Angela and Oliver. "I should have anticipated—"

"Not your fault," Angela replied, though her expression remained grim. "Some people are simply determined to make every interaction about their personal grievances."

After we returned to the fair proper, I noticed Gary had resumed his position at his makeshift truth booth, but his earlier evangelical fervor had been replaced by sullen determination. Several fairgoers gave his table a wide berth, apparently having learned to recognize the warning signs of his conspiracy lectures.

"He's running out of audience," Beau observed, following my gaze. "That's when people like Gary become most dangerous when they realize their message isn't being received the way they expected."

The rest of the afternoon proceeded with cautious normalcy. Authors gave their scheduled readings, browsers purchased books, and the fair maintained its literary atmosphere despite the morning's disruptions. But I couldn't shake the feeling that Gary's increasingly isolated position was building toward something more serious than public embarrassment.

By five o'clock, most of the day's attendees had

dispersed, leaving only the evening program participants and a few dedicated browsers. Gary had finally abandoned his truth booth, though I noticed his white Ford was still parked near the village hall.

"Has anyone seen Gary recently?" I asked Malcolm as we began closing down the day's activities.

"Not for the past hour," Malcolm replied. "Though his materials are still on that table, so presumably he intends to return."

Both dogs had maintained their unusual alertness all afternoon, occasionally lifting their heads to scan the fair as if searching for a specific threat. Their behavior was beginning to make me genuinely nervous.

"Maybe he's finally given up for the day," Freya suggested hopefully.

But even as she spoke, both Austen and Hardy suddenly stood up, their attention focused on something across the green. Following their gaze, I could see that the lights were on in Oliver's shop, though it should have been closed for the day.

"That's odd," I murmured. "Oliver usually closes at four on Saturdays."

A moment later, we heard it—a scream, sharp and terrified, coming from Oliver's antique shop.

Without thinking, I ran toward the sound with both dogs racing beside me, their protective instincts overriding everything else. Behind me, I could hear Beau, Malcolm, and Freya following, but my attention was focused entirely on reaching whatever had caused that awful sound.

The front door of Oliver's shop stood ajar, revealing the darkened interior beyond. I pushed through it without hesitation, calling out, "Oliver? Is everything all right?"

No answer.

The shop felt wrong. Too quiet, too still, and both dogs pressed close to my legs rather than investigating as they usually would.

"Oliver?" I called again, making my way through the maze of antique furniture toward the consultation room at the back.

The door to the workshop room was closed, but light leaked from beneath it. I reached for the handle, then hesitated as both dogs suddenly sat down and refused to move closer.

"Ginny?" Beau's voice came from behind me. "What's wrong?"

"The dogs won't go near the workshop room," I said quietly. "Something's wrong."

Beau moved past me to the door, paused for a moment, then pushed it open.

"Dear God," he said quietly, then immediately stepped back, blocking my view. "Ginny, we need to call the police. Now."

But I could already see past him into the workshop room, and the sight made my knees weak.

Gary Stephens lay sprawled on the floor beside the consultation table, his conspiracy papers scattered around him like fallen leaves. A brass letter opener protruded from his chest, and his eyes stared sightlessly at the ceiling with an expression of complete surprise.

His manila folder lay open beside him, its contents finally spilled for all to see. But Gary would never again explain to anyone how the literary establishment really operated.

The Tidehaven Cove Literary Fair had just become a crime scene.

7

"Don't touch anything," I said automatically, stepping back from the doorway. The sight of Gary's body brought back unwelcome memories of finding Dr. Thornbury in my rare book room just months ago. "We need to call the police and secure the scene."

"Should I call 911?" Beau asked, reaching for his phone.

"999," I corrected, already dialing. "And we need to ask for CID. This isn't something for the local constable." At least this time I knew the procedure.

Both dogs had retreated to the far end of the shop, pressing themselves against a Victorian wardrobe as if trying to disappear. Hardy was whimpering softly, while Austen sat frozen with her ears flat against her head.

"999, what's your emergency?" The operator's voice was professionally calm.

"We need police and an ambulance at Blackthorn Antiques in Tidehaven Cove," I managed, surprised by how steady my own voice sounded. "There's been a... there's a dead body."

"Are you certain the person is deceased?"

I looked toward the workshop room, where Gary's still form was visible through the doorway. "Yes. Very certain."

"Right, we'll have units dispatched immediately. Can you secure the scene and ensure no one enters or leaves the premises?"

"Yes, we can do that."

As I ended the call, Malcolm and Freya appeared in the shop entrance, both looking pale and shaken.

"Is it true?" Freya whispered. "Is it Gary?"

"Don't come any closer," I warned, echoing what I'd learned from my previous murder scene experience. "We need to preserve everything for the police."

Malcolm's face had gone ashen. "But how? What happened?"

"We don't know," I replied. "We just found him."

"Where's Oliver?" Freya asked, looking around the empty shop. "This is his building; he should be here."

That was a disturbing point I hadn't considered. Oliver's shop, Oliver's workshop room, but no Oliver in sight. "I don't know. His car's not outside."

"The shop should be closed by now," Malcolm said slowly. "How did Gary get inside? Oliver always locks up at four on Saturdays."

"Maybe Oliver let him in?" Freya suggested. "For a private discussion after the workshop disaster?"

"Or Gary had a key somehow," Beau said grimly.

"Should we try calling Oliver?" I asked, pulling out my phone again.

I dialed Oliver's number, but it went straight to voicemail. "Oliver, it's Ginny. There's been an incident at your shop. Please call me back immediately."

"We need to account for everyone who was at the fair today," Beau said grimly. "Starting with everyone who had conflicts with Gary."

"That's practically the entire guest list," Malcolm pointed out with dark humor.

Within minutes, we could hear sirens approaching, first the ambulance, then police cars. The peaceful afternoon atmosphere of the literary fair was shattered as emergency vehicles pulled up outside Oliver's shop, their flashing lights drawing curious villagers from their Saturday activities.

Constable Peter Trewin arrived first, his usually relaxed demeanor replaced by professional alertness as he surveyed the scene. "Right then, what do we have?"

"Dead body in the back workshop room," I reported. "Gary Stephens, one of our fair attendees. We found him about ten minutes ago."

"Anyone else in the building when you arrived?"

"No. The front door was ajar, but the shop appeared empty except for..." I gestured toward the back room.

"Right. Everyone needs to step outside while we secure the scene." Constable Trewin began stringing police tape across the shop entrance. "Detective Inspector will want to speak with all of you, but for now, please wait across the green."

As we moved away from Oliver's shop, I noticed that word of the incident was already spreading through the village. Small groups of fairgoers had gathered at safe distances, speaking in hushed voices while casting worried glances toward the police activity.

"Poor Gary," Freya said quietly as we settled on a bench near the village green. "I know he was difficult, but nobody deserves..."

"No," I agreed, though I had to admit my first emotion had been shock rather than grief. Gary had made himself so universally disliked that it was hard to feel genuine sorrow about his death.

Both dogs had gradually calmed down as we moved away from the crime scene, though they remained closer to me than usual. Hardy settled against my legs with a soft sigh, while Austen crept closer to the police. I called her back before anyone noticed.

"Who do you think screamed?" Malcolm asked suddenly. "We heard someone scream, but Gary was already... and Oliver wasn't there."

"Good question," Beau said thoughtfully. "Someone else must have discovered the body before we arrived. Or..."

"Or the killer screamed when they realized what they'd done," I finished.

The implications of that possibility hung in the air as we watched more police cars arrive. A familiar figure in a dark suit emerged from one of them, Detective Inspector Drake, who had investigated Dr. Thornbury's murder at my bookshop just months earlier.

"Ms. Hampton," DI Drake said, approaching our little group with a look that was part recognition, part resignation. "I should have known you'd be involved when we got the call about a body at a literary event."

DI Drake was a woman in her early forties with short auburn hair and sharp green eyes that seemed to take in everything at once. She wore a practical navy suit and comfortable shoes, looking like she'd dealt with plenty of village crimes before.

"Right," she said, consulting a notebook. "I'll need to speak with each of you individually, but first, who can give me a basic timeline of events?"

"Gary Stephens was attending a manuscript critique workshop in Oliver Blackthorn's consultation room," I began. "The workshop was scheduled from two to four, led by Angela Victor. There was some kind of disturbance around three-thirty. We heard arguing and what sounded like something crashing."

"Where was Mr. Blackthorn during this workshop?"

"He was there when we investigated the disturbance," I said. "In the consultation room with Angela when the workshop fell apart. But I don't know when he left or where he went after that."

"And when did you discover the body?"

Her businesslike questions helped calm my nerves. "About twenty minutes ago. We heard a scream and ran to investigate. The front door was open, the shop was empty except for... Gary."

DI Drake made careful notes. "I'll need to speak with this Angela Victor and Oliver Blackthorn immediately. Are they still on the premises?"

"Angela was helping with the evening setup last I saw," Freya offered. "But I haven't seen Oliver since the workshop ended."

"His car's not in its usual spot," Malcolm added helpfully. "Silver Jaguar, registration—"

"We'll find him," DI Drake interrupted. "For now, I need all of you to remain available for individual interviews. Don't discuss the case among yourselves, and don't leave the village without checking with us first."

As the detective inspector moved away to organize the crime scene investigation, the four of us sat in uncomfortable silence on the bench. The literary fair continued around us in subdued fashion, though the police presence had clearly dampened the afternoon's enthusiasm.

"I can't believe this has happened," I said finally. "A murder at our book fair."

"At least it wasn't in your shop," Malcolm pointed out with dark practicality. "Though I suppose that's small comfort."

8

The village hall had been transformed into a makeshift incident room, with police officers bustling about and the weekend's cheerful literary atmosphere replaced by something altogether more serious. But I wasn't summoned there immediately, instead, DI Drake found me at the information booth, looking like she could use a proper cup of tea and a moment away from official procedures.

"Ms. Hampton," she said, approaching with what might have been relief. "I wonder if we could have a chat? Somewhere a bit more comfortable than that converted hall."

"Of course. The bookshop's quieter, and Malcolm always keeps the tea on." I glanced around at the subdued fairgoers, many of whom were packing up early. "This isn't exactly how I planned to end our literary weekend."

"I imagine not." DI Drake fell into step beside me, while both dogs trotted along as unofficial escorts. "Though I have to say, when we got the call about a murder at a literary event in Tidehaven Cove, your name was the first one I thought of."

"I seem to have developed a talent for finding bodies," I replied with weak humor. "Though I promise it's not intentional."

"I'm sure it isn't." There was definitely amusement in her eyes now. "At least you can keep your fair going. Helps keep everyone conveniently gathered for questioning."

The bookshop felt wonderfully normal after the chaos outside. Malcolm was already bustling about with the tea service, having anticipated our arrival and knowing the miraculous effect tea had in a crisis.

"Detective Inspector," he said formally, though his tone was warm. "I saw you coming over and got out the good china. I thought you might need proper refreshments after such a trying afternoon."

"That's very thoughtful, thank you." DI Drake settled into one of the comfortable reading chairs near the fiction section, while both dogs immediately appointed themselves supervisors of the proceedings.

I busied myself helping Malcolm with the tea, finding the familiar ritual of warming the pot and arranging biscuits oddly soothing. "You mentioned wanting a chat rather than a formal interview?"

"Well, I'll need an official statement eventually, but right now I could use someone who understands what's been happening here." DI Drake accepted her cup with obvious gratitude. "Tell me about Gary Stephens. How well did you know him?"

"Hardly at all. He bought his ticket online. I didn't even know his name until he showed up Friday morning." I settled into the chair across from her, with Hardy immediately claiming the spot by my feet. "But he started causing problems almost immediately."

"What sort of problems?"

As I described Gary's weekend of disruption, from the children's story time to his various confrontations with publishing professionals, Malcolm nodded along while arranging more biscuits on the plate.

"He did seem rather... intense about his theories," Malcolm observed diplomatically. "Though I suppose some authors are quite passionate about their work."

"Passionate is one word for it," I agreed. "Gary was convinced that any criticism of his manuscript proved there was a conspiracy against him personally."

The shop bell chimed, and Freya appeared looking like a whirlwind had passed through her hair, carrying what looked like a plate of sandwiches from the tea shop.

"I thought you might need sustenance," she announced, then paused when she saw DI Drake. "Oh! Sorry, I didn't mean to interrupt."

"Please, come in," DI Drake said warmly. "I could use all the local perspective I can get."

"You remember Freya," I said, making introductions while Freya settled into the remaining chair. "Freya's been helping coordinate the fair, so she's seen all the same interactions I have."

"Excellent. So Gary Stephens managed to antagonize most of your publishing professionals?"

"Pretty much everyone," Freya confirmed, accepting tea from Malcolm. "Authors, agents, publishers, even Oliver who was just renting out workshop space. Gary had this talent for attacking people exactly where it would hurt most professionally."

DI Drake made notes between sips of tea, occasionally pausing to give Hardy an absent pat when he nudged her knee hopefully.

"Tell me about the manuscript workshop where the final disturbance occurred," she said.

I described the confrontation between Gary and Angela Victor, his insistence that editorial advice was a form of censorship, and Angela's eventual decision to eject him from the session.

"Was Oliver Blackthorn leading that workshop?" DI Drake asked.

"Oh no," Freya jumped in. "Angela was running the session. She was renting Oliver's back room because we needed the space. Oliver was there because the shop is full of valuable antiques. Angela was in charge of the actual critique."

"I see. And after Gary left?"

"He went back to his conspiracy booth for a while," I said. "Then he just... vanished. We didn't see him again until we found him."

Malcolm appeared at DI Drake's elbow with the teapot. "More tea, Inspector? And perhaps a sandwich? You look as though you haven't eaten properly today."

"You're very kind, thank you." DI Drake accepted both gratefully. "It's refreshing to have a proper break. Police work doesn't often allow for civilized tea service."

"Malcolm believes all of life's problems can be improved with proper tea," I said fondly. "He's usually right."

"Quite right too," DI Drake agreed, then turned back to business. "Now, about when you discovered the body. You heard a scream?"

"Yes, but the shop was empty when we got there. Just Gary in the workshop room." I paused, thinking. "That scream still puzzles me. Who made it, and where did they go?"

"That's one of several questions I'm working on," DI

Drake said, making another note. "Tell me about your friend Mr. Morrison. Convenient timing for his visit."

"Beau came for the fair weekend. We worked together in Charleston before I inherited the bookshop." I could hear the slight defensiveness in my voice and tried to soften it. "He's been looking forward to this trip for months."

"I'm sure. Though his publishing background does make him... interesting from an investigative standpoint."

The shop bell chimed again, and this time it was Mrs. Patterson from the flower shop, looking flustered and apologetic.

"Oh, I'm so sorry to interrupt," she said, taking in our little tea party. "I just wanted to check that everything was all right. Such terrible goings-on for our lovely village."

"Please, don't apologize," DI Drake said kindly. "I'm Detective Inspector Drake. Were you at the fair this weekend?"

"Oh yes, wouldn't have missed it. Though I have to say, that Gary fellow gave me the shivers from the first moment I saw him." Mrs. Patterson settled into the chair Malcolm quickly provided. "Always muttering and waving those papers about. My late husband used to say you could spot trouble coming a mile away if you knew what to look for."

"Did you happen to notice anything unusual yesterday evening?" DI Drake asked with professional interest.

"Well, now that you mention it, I did see someone near Oliver's shop around teatime. Couldn't make out who it was from my window, but they seemed to be in quite a hurry."

After Mrs. Patterson left with a book on flower arranging and a promise to "keep an eye out for anything suspicious," DI Drake turned back to me with a slight smile.

"This is much more civilized than interviewing people in

a converted village hall," she said. "You get a better sense of the community dynamics over proper tea."

"We do try to look after each other," I agreed. "Even when we're harboring murderers, apparently."

"About that," DI Drake said, her expression growing more serious. "I think I'm going to need your help with this investigation. You understand these people and their relationships in ways I don't. The publishing world has some rather complex dynamics that I'm still trying to grasp."

"I'll do whatever I can," I said. "Though I have to admit, I never expected my second literary fair to turn into a murder investigation."

"Life has a way of surprising us," DI Drake agreed, finishing her tea and standing. "Thank you for the hospitality. It's made a difficult day considerably more pleasant."

"At least someone's happy with how today turned out," I observed, watching Malcolm arrange the china with particular care.

"Well," he said with just a hint of pride, "it's not often we get to show proper village hospitality to someone official. Standards must be maintained, even during murder investigations."

9

M alcolm appeared at the bookshop door just as I was unlocking it for the fair's final day, his usually impeccable appearance showing signs of strain.

"Good morning, Miss Hampton," he said formally, though his voice carried an undercurrent of worry. "I'm afraid there's been another development."

"What now?" I asked, dreading the answer while both dogs pressed close to my legs. The steady drizzle outside seemed to match everyone's subdued mood.

"The police have tracked down Sarah Pemberton," Malcolm replied. "She's on her way back from London for questioning. Apparently her urgent business yesterday was somewhat less urgent than she claimed."

Beau approached from across the green, looking unusually tired. "What kind of business?" he asked.

"According to Constable Trewin, she claimed to have a client emergency requiring immediate attention," Malcolm said. "But when the police checked with her agency, no such emergency existed. She simply left without explanation."

That didn't look good for Sarah. As one of Gary's primary antagonists, her convenient departure just before the murder was discovered would put her squarely in DI Drake's crosshairs.

"Poor Sarah," I said, though I wasn't entirely sure I meant it. Her confrontation with Gary had been genuinely unpleasant to witness.

"Poor Sarah nothing," Freya said, appearing behind Malcolm with her hair plastered to her head from the rain. "Did you see how she spoke to him yesterday? I thought she was going to physically throw him out of her session."

That was true. Sarah's "meet the agent" workshop had turned into a public humiliation when Gary insisted on pitching his conspiracy thriller despite her obvious disinterest.

"Gary did ambush her with his manuscript," Beau pointed out fairly. "She was probably just trying to maintain professional boundaries."

"By calling his work 'unpublishable drivel' in front of half the fair?" Freya countered. "That wasn't professional boundaries, that was character assassination."

I remembered the scene clearly. Gary had cornered Sarah during her submission guidelines presentation, waving his manila folder and demanding she explain why agents were suppressing political fiction. Sarah's initial attempts at diplomacy had quickly dissolved into cutting dismissal when Gary refused to accept her editorial feedback.

"He was persistent," Malcolm said with British under-statement. "Though perhaps Ms. Pemberton's response was somewhat... vigorous."

That was putting it mildly. Sarah had eventually lost her temper completely, telling Gary that his manuscript read like "paranoid rambling" and that he should "try writing actual fiction instead of conspiracy theories masquerading as literature."

The public nature of the confrontation had clearly humiliated Gary, though he'd covered his embarrassment with his usual claims about establishment suppression. But I'd seen the hurt in his eyes beneath the bluster.

"She does have a motive," I admitted reluctantly. "Gary was damaging her professional reputation by association. Having someone like that disrupting your workshop reflects badly on your judgment."

"Exactly," Freya said. "And agents live and die by their reputations. One difficult client can poison relationships with editors and publishers."

That was a good point. Sarah Pemberton Literary Associates was a respected agency, and Sarah's client list included several bestselling authors. Having Gary publicly attack her credibility and editorial standards could have serious professional consequences.

"But murder?" Beau asked skeptically. "Over a difficult manuscript submission?"

"I'm sure you know that people have killed for less," Malcolm observed darkly. "Particularly when their livelihood is threatened."

"I should get the shop properly opened," I said, noting how the police presence across the green had changed the fair's atmosphere. Even from here, I could see that conversations were more subdued, browsers moved more cautiously, and several authors looked like they'd rather be anywhere else.

"I'll handle the morning setup," Malcolm offered. "You should probably check on the other participants."

"There's Angela," Freya said, nodding toward the poetry

corner where Angela Victor was setting up for the morning's workshop. "She looks terrible."

Angela did look strained, her usual confidence replaced by obvious worry as she arranged papers with shaking hands. As the workshop leader who'd ejected Gary, she was probably feeling the weight of police scrutiny.

"I should go talk to her," I decided. "Make sure she's holding up okay."

Angela looked up as I approached, her smile forced and bright. "Ginny! How are you managing with all this drama?"

"I'm fine. How are you doing? Yesterday must have been horrible."

"It was rather awful," Angela admitted, her composure cracking slightly. "Gary was so... intense about his theories. I've dealt with difficult writers before, but his level of delusion was genuinely unsettling."

"DI Drake hasn't been too hard on you, I hope?"

"Professional but thorough," Angela replied diplomatically, reaching down to give Hardy a distracted pat as he sniffed around her workshop materials. "Though I have to say, being treated as a murder suspect isn't exactly how I planned to spend my weekend."

I could understand her distress. Angela was a respected author with a solid reputation in domestic fiction. Being connected to a murder investigation, even as a witness, could damage her carefully built career.

"The police have to check everyone," I said reassuringly. "I'm sure they'll clear you quickly."

"I hope so. Though I have to admit, Gary's behavior yesterday was so disruptive that I genuinely wanted to throttle him myself." Angela paused, then looked horrified. "Oh God, I shouldn't say things like that, should I? Not with the police investigating."

"They understand that people get frustrated with difficult personalities," I assured her. "That's different from actually acting on those feelings."

But even as I said it, I wondered if that was true. Gary had been so universally annoying that almost everyone at the fair had expressed some form of violent sentiment about him. The question was which of those expressions had been mere frustration and which had been genuine intent.

"Have you seen Oliver?" Angela asked, changing the subject. "It's so strange that he's just disappeared."

"No one's heard from him. The police are trying to track him down."

"It does look rather suspicious, doesn't it? His shop, his workshop room, and then he vanishes just when Gary turns up dead." Angela shivered despite the mild weather. "I keep thinking about how angry he was when Gary questioned his authentication methods. Oliver takes his professional reputation very seriously."

That was another good point. Oliver's confrontation with Gary had been particularly bitter, with Gary essentially accusing him of fraud and intellectual dishonesty. For someone whose business depended on credibility and expertise, that kind of public attack could be devastating.

"Everyone's under suspicion until the police sort this out," I said. "The important thing is to keep the fair going and try to maintain some normalcy."

"Normalcy," Angela repeated with a bitter laugh. "At a book fair with a murder investigation. I suppose stranger things have happened, but I can't think where."

10

I was restocking the display table when Marcus Webb approached with a steaming cup of tea from Elspeth's stall, looking like a man who'd spent the night staring at the ceiling rather than sleeping.

"Miss Hampton," he said with a rueful smile. "Might I have a word? About Friday night's little drama at the pub."

"Of course," I replied, noting how both dogs immediately positioned themselves between Marcus and me. They'd been unusually protective since Gary's murder, though Hardy seemed more interested in the possibility that Marcus might drop some biscuit crumbs.

Marcus glanced around at the fair's subdued but continuing bustle, browsers still examining books despite the police tape visible across the green, children still queuing for story time, Elspeth still serving tea with determined cheerfulness.

"I suppose you've heard what happened," he said, settling onto a nearby bench. "Gary's little performance at the pub Friday night."

"Something about publishing conspiracy theories?"

"Rather more than that, I'm afraid." Marcus sipped his tea thoughtfully. "He spent the better part of an hour explaining to anyone who'd listen why independent publishers like me are actually the most insidious part of the literary establishment."

"How so?" I asked, genuinely curious despite myself.

"According to Gary, we pretend to be brave and independent while actually publishing 'safe rebellion' books that make readers feel enlightened without challenging anything truly dangerous." Marcus's tone was more bemused than bitter. "Apparently I'm part of a vast conspiracy to control what people think by giving them the illusion of radical literature."

That did sound like Gary's brand of paranoid logic. "But surely people who read your books know they enjoy them," I said. "That's what really matters, isn't it?"

"You'd think so. But Gary had charts, Miss Hampton. Actual diagrams showing supposed connections between independent presses and mainstream publishers. He made it sound quite convincing, really." Marcus managed a wry smile. "I have to admire his thoroughness, even if his conclusions were complete nonsense."

Both dogs had settled at my feet, with Austen keeping a watchful eye on Marcus while Hardy dozed in the morning sun filtering through the clouds.

Gary's obsession had taken over everyone's better sense. I suppose it was inevitable, squeaky wheel and all that. "When did things get heated?"

"When he started approaching my authors directly, people I've worked with for years, asking if they knew their publisher was suppressing their 'real' political messages." Marcus shook his head with what seemed more like exhaustion than anger. "That's when I rather lost my temper."

"What did you say?"

"Probably more than I should have. Something about authors who blame publishers for their own shortcomings, and perhaps the problem wasn't institutional suppression but simply poor writing." Marcus winced slightly. "Not my finest moment of diplomacy."

"I imagine that didn't go over well."

"Gary started lecturing the entire pub about elitist gatekeeping and academic bias. Got quite worked up, really. The landlord had to step in before things got completely out of hand."

Across the green, I noticed a familiar figure emerging from a taxi near the village hall. Sarah Pemberton, looking considerably less polished than when she'd left yesterday. Her usually perfect hair was windblown, and she looked like she was dreading what came next.

"Looks like Sarah's back," I observed.

Marcus followed my gaze and grimaced. "Poor woman. Though I suppose we're all going to face uncomfortable questions before this is over."

"The police have spoken to you already?"

"Yesterday evening. Very thorough, DI Drake. Asked about my finances, my relationship with Gary, whether I'd seen him after Friday night." Marcus's tone remained conversational, but I caught an undercurrent of worry. "I think she suspects I might have killed him to protect my business reputation."

"Did you see him after Friday?"

"Briefly, Saturday morning. He was setting up that conspiracy display of his, looking quite pleased with himself." Marcus sighed. "I may have suggested that his behavior was damaging innocent people and that he should consider the consequences."

That was brave. "How did he respond?"

"Laughed, actually. Said people who profited from deception always got upset when someone exposed uncomfortable truths." Marcus finished his tea and stood up, looking more resigned than defeated. "He was completely unrepentant about the whole thing."

"Marcus, you didn't go to Oliver's shop yesterday evening, did you?"

"Good heavens, no. I was at the B&B making damage control phone calls to authors who'd heard about Gary's accusations." He paused. "Though I don't suppose I can prove that, can I?"

As Marcus walked away with a friendly wave to the dogs, I found myself thinking that while he certainly had reason to dislike Gary, he seemed more like someone who'd respond to crisis with worried phone calls than violent action.

Still, as I'd learned from my previous experience with village murders, even the most unlikely people were capable of surprising things when their livelihoods were threatened.

11

Diana Hartwell was signing books at her table near the tea shop when I approached, her usual polished composure intact despite the morning's drizzle and police presence. A small queue of devoted readers clutched well-worn paperbacks, chattering excitedly about her latest thriller while Diana smiled and spoke with each person. I was struck by how little Gary's death seemed to have affected her fans. They were completely absorbed in discussing plot twists and favorite characters, as if there wasn't a murder investigation happening fifty yards away.

"How are you holding up?" I asked during a brief lull between fans.

"As well as can be expected," Diana replied, her voice carrying just a hint of strain. "Though I have to say, this isn't quite how I imagined my weekend in Devon would go."

Priya appeared at Diana's elbow with a fresh cup of coffee and a concerned expression. "The police want to interview you again this afternoon," she said quietly. "Something about Saturday's workshop incident."

"Ah yes, Gary's little performance." Diana's smile was

diplomatic but tired. "I suppose they need to understand what happened during that craft session."

I remembered the scene clearly. Gary's increasingly aggressive challenges to Diana's teaching methods, his insistence that her structural advice was designed to suppress political content, and the way he'd dominated the discussion until other participants began looking uncomfortable.

"He really did disrupt the entire workshop," I said sympathetically.

"More than disrupted," Priya interjected with obvious frustration. "He completely derailed what was supposed to be a discussion of pacing techniques. Some of those people had paid good money to learn from Diana, not to listen to conspiracy theories about publishing suppression."

Diana laid a gentle hand on her assistant's arm. "It's all right, Priya. These things happen at literary events."

"But it's not all right," Priya continued, her purple hair catching the light as she shook her head. "He was incredibly rude to you in front of your readers. That woman who'd driven all the way from Cornwall specifically for your workshop looked ready to ask for her money back."

"Actually," I said, "would it help if we offered a make-up session? Maybe a Zoom workshop for the people who didn't get the experience they came for?"

Diana's face brightened slightly. "That's very thoughtful of you. I'd be happy to do something like that once this mess is sorted out."

Both dogs had followed me over and now sat politely beside Diana's table, with Hardy watching hopefully as Diana opened a small bag of sweets while Austen observed the steady stream of fairgoers with alert interest.

"What exactly did Gary say during the workshop?" I asked, suddenly wishing I'd found a way to be in every event all the time. I knew the answer would be a familiar tale, but perhaps something had happened before I arrived.

"The usual theories about craft advice being a form of censorship," Diana replied wearily. "He seemed convinced that my suggestions about character development and plot structure were designed to make political fiction 'safe' for mainstream consumption."

"He kept interrupting her," Priya added, clearly still upset about the incident. "Every time Diana tried to explain a concept, he'd launch into another lecture about how traditional storytelling techniques were meant to distract readers from real issues. Some people actually left early."

That was damaging indeed. Diana's reputation as a workshop leader was an important part of her career, and having participants walk out would reflect badly on her abilities as an instructor.

"I tried to redirect the discussion," Diana said diplomatically. "But Gary was quite passionate about his theories. He seemed to genuinely believe that anyone offering writing advice was part of some vast conspiracy to control literature."

"The worst part was when he started questioning your credibility as a thriller writer," Priya said, her voice rising slightly. "Suggesting that your success proved you were writing 'establishment-approved' fiction instead of real political commentary."

I could see why that would be particularly galling. Diana had built her career on intelligent, well-researched thrillers that often tackled serious social issues. Having someone dismiss her work as propaganda would be deeply insulting.

"How did you respond to that?" I asked.

"Professionally," Diana replied, though something flickered in her eyes. "I explained that successful fiction often explores political themes through character and story rather than direct polemic. But Gary wasn't interested in nuance."

"He basically accused her of selling out for commercial success," Priya said bluntly. "Right in front of people who'd come specifically to meet their favorite author. It was humiliating."

Diana's next fan approached with a shy smile and a stack of books to sign, temporarily ending our conversation. As Diana chatted warmly with the reader about her latest novel, I noticed how quickly her professional mask slipped back into place.

"She's been doing this all morning," Priya said quietly. "Smiling and being gracious while the police treat her like a suspect. Do you know they asked about her 'access' to workshop areas yesterday evening? As if she'd sneak around stabbing people with letter openers."

"They have to investigate everyone who had conflicts with Gary," I said reasonably.

"But Diana didn't have a conflict with him," Priya protested. "She handled his disruption professionally and tried to keep the workshop on track. If anyone should be a suspect, it's that antiques dealer who actually threw Gary out of his space."

"You mean Oliver?"

"Right. He was furious about Gary questioning his authentication methods. Much angrier than Diana ever got." Priya glanced around nervously. "Though I suppose I shouldn't be pointing fingers at other people."

"Did you see Gary after the workshop ended?"

Priya hesitated just long enough to make me curious. "Briefly. I was collecting the feedback forms from various workshop rooms around five o'clock. Gary was... still upset about being ejected from Oliver's session."

"Where did you see him?"

"Near the tea shop. He was muttering something about establishment gatekeepers and how he'd prove his point eventually." Priya's voice dropped. "To be honest, he seemed a bit unhinged. Like someone who might do something desperate."

That was an interesting perspective. Gary as potentially dangerous rather than just annoying. "Did he say anything specific?"

"Something about having evidence that would expose the whole conspiracy. He was clutching that manila folder of his like it contained state secrets." Priya shuddered slightly. "I was actually relieved when he walked away. There was something in his eyes that was genuinely unsettling."

12

The poetry corner had become oddly popular since the murder, with fairgoers clustering around the display as if violent death had made them suddenly philosophical. I was watching this unexpected literary revival when Elliot approached, looking slightly out of place among the book browsers.

"How are you holding up?" he asked, his voice carrying the gentle concern I'd come to associate with his professional manner.

"Surviving," I replied, grateful for his steady presence. "Though this isn't exactly how I imagined my second literary fair would go. The first one was just authors reading poetry and people buying books. Much more peaceful."

Both dogs immediately trotted over to greet him, tails wagging with obvious delight. Elliot crouched down to give them proper attention, and I noticed how they both relaxed in his presence, clearly viewing him as a source of calm in the current chaos.

"I've been thinking about yesterday," he said, straightening up and glancing around at the subdued but continuing fair. "About Gary and his... theories. There might be something I can help with."

"Oh?" I tried to keep my tone neutral, though I couldn't imagine what veterinary expertise might contribute to a literary murder investigation.

"Well, I've dealt with similar personality types in my practice," Elliot continued earnestly. "Obsessive clients who develop elaborate theories about pharmaceutical conspiracies or believe that veterinary medicine is controlled by corporate interests."

Freya looked up from her book arranging with obvious interest. "I've met the type at university. People who think being critical makes them intellectually superior. But Gary was the worst example I've ever seen."

"Similar patterns, yes. Paranoid thinking, persecution complexes, the conviction that any professional advice is actually a form of control or suppression." Elliot spoke carefully, as if explaining a diagnosis. "In my experience, people like that often escalate their behavior when they feel cornered."

"What kind of escalation?" I asked, though I suspected this might not be as helpful as Elliot hoped.

"Increased aggression, more public confrontations, sometimes threats against the people they believe are suppressing them." He paused thoughtfully. "Has anyone checked whether Gary made any direct threats against specific individuals?"

"I think the police are looking into that," I said diplomatically. The truth was, Gary had been so generally hostile to everyone that specific threats would be hard to distinguish from his usual conspiracy rants.

"The thing is," Elliot continued, warming to his theme, "in veterinary medicine we see this kind of thinking when people can't accept that their pet's illness isn't caused by some vast pharmaceutical conspiracy. They'd rather believe in secret corporate control than accept that sometimes animals just get sick."

Beau approached from the direction of the village hall, looking thoughtful. "Interesting theory," he said, having caught the end of Elliot's explanation. "Though in Gary's case, the publishing industry dynamics are a bit more complex than veterinary medicine."

I caught the subtle edge in Beau's tone and noticed Elliot's slight stiffening in response.

"Of course," Elliot replied with careful politeness. "I'm sure your expertise in publishing gives you better insight into Gary's specific delusions."

"Well, the manuscript submission process can be genuinely frustrating for authors," Beau said smoothly. "Though most people don't develop elaborate conspiracy theories about it."

"Right," Elliot said, though his tone suggested he wasn't entirely convinced. "I was just thinking that if we understood Gary's psychological pattern, it might help identify who he was most likely to target."

"That's actually not a bad idea," Freya interjected, apparently oblivious to the competitive atmosphere. "Gary did seem to focus his anger on specific people rather than just ranting generally."

"Exactly," Elliot said, looking pleased that someone appreciated his contribution. "In animal behavior, we call it 'redirected aggression' —when an animal can't reach its primary target, it attacks something else instead."

"So you think Gary might have been targeting someone specific?" I asked.

"Possibly. Or he might have been building up to a

confrontation with whoever he saw as his main enemy." Elliot paused, clearly trying to apply his veterinary knowledge to human psychology. "The question is whether he actually initiated that confrontation, or if someone decided to silence him first."

Beau was studying Elliot with newfound interest. "That's actually quite perceptive. Gary's behavior did seem to be escalating rather than just maintaining the same level of annoyance."

"Thank you," Elliot said, though he sounded more surprised than pleased by Beau's approval.

Malcolm appeared at my elbow with perfect timing. "Miss Hampton, DI Drake would like to speak with you again. I must say she sounded quite exhausted on the phone. I don't envy her the job of dealing with such awful people."

As I prepared to head back to the village hall, I noticed both men watching me with expressions I couldn't quite interpret. Elliot looked genuinely concerned, while Beau seemed more thoughtful.

"I could come with you," Elliot offered. "For moral support."

"That's kind of you, but I think DI Drake prefers to interview people individually," I replied gently.

"Of course. Though if you need anything afterward..." He trailed off, clearly feeling the awkwardness of not quite belonging to the literary world that had become the center of this crisis.

"I'll be fine," I assured him. "But thank you for the insights about Gary's behavior pattern. That actually was helpful." Both dogs chose to accompany me toward the village hall, apparently deciding that police interviews required their protective presence.

As we walked away, I could hear Elliot and Beau continuing their conversation about Gary's psychological profile, their voices gradually becoming more collaborative and less competitive. Perhaps a murder investigation was exactly what they needed to find common ground.

13

I strode toward the temporary incident room, stopping here and there to talk to readers and vendors. I couldn't shirk my duties as organizer after all. Before I made it, DI Drake appeared two steaming cups from Elspeth's tea stall in hand and wearing an expression that suggested she was ready for a proper conversation rather than an official interrogation.

"Ms. Hampton," she said, offering me one of the cups with what was definitely a smile this time. "I wonder if you might spare a few minutes? Not for an interview this time. I could use your perspective on a few things, and I suspect we could both use a break from all the official procedures."

"Of course," I said, accepting the tea gratefully. The warm ceramic felt wonderful in my hands, and the familiar aroma of Elspeth's special Sunday blend was exactly what I needed. Both dogs immediately positioned themselves nearby, apparently deciding that informal chats with police still required their careful supervision, though Hardy's tail wagging suggested he approved of this more relaxed approach.

"Walk with me?" DI Drake gestured toward the quieter end of the green, away from the fair's continuing bustle. "I've spent the morning interviewing suspects in that converted village hall, and frankly, I could use some fresh air and a friendly face. Plus, I'm finding that the publishing world has some rather complex dynamics I don't fully understand."

"It can be incredibly complicated," I agreed, falling into step beside her while Austen and Hardy flanked us like tiny bodyguards. "So many professional relationships and careers at stake. Everyone's reputation matters, but in different ways."

We made our way past the poetry corner, where a small crowd had gathered around a local author reading from her latest collection, their faces lit with the particular pleasure that comes from hearing beautiful words spoken aloud. The afternoon light was golden and warm, making even our serious conversation feel less ominous.

"Exactly what I'm struggling with," DI Drake said as we settled on the bench overlooking the harbor. "Gary Stephens seems to have had an impressive talent for attacking people precisely where it would hurt most professionally. It's like he had a map of everyone's vulnerabilities."

I sipped my tea thoughtfully, watching a small fishing boat make its way back to harbor while Hardy investigated some particularly interesting seaweed that had washed up nearby. "Gary was very good at finding people's weak spots, wasn't he? Though I don't think it was intentional. He was just so focused on his conspiracy theories that he attacked anything that contradicted them."

"Tell me," DI Drake continued, her voice taking on a more conversational tone, "in your experience with the publishing world, which of these conflicts would be serious enough to drive someone to murder? I need to understand what we're really dealing with here."

I considered the question carefully, aware that my answer might help shape the direction of her investigation. "Well, take Sarah Pemberton. Her credibility as an agent is absolutely crucial to her business, it's everything, really. Having someone publicly question her editorial judgment in front of potential clients could cost her existing authors and damage her relationships with publishers. That's not just professional embarrassment, that's career destruction."

"Interesting that you mention Sarah first," DI Drake observed. "She's back from London, by the way. Claims she left because of a family emergency that turned out to be a false alarm—her elderly mother thought she was having chest pains, but it was just indigestion from too much rich food at a neighbor's birthday party." Her tone was carefully neutral. "Convenient timing, but certainly possible. Emergency calls from elderly parents rarely follow convenient schedules."

"What about Marcus Webb?" I asked, thinking of the publisher's obvious distress after Gary's pub confrontation.

"Now that's an interesting case," DI Drake said, warming to the subject. "He's genuinely distraught about the potential damage to his press's standing. Says Gary's accusations about publishing 'controlled opposition' could destroy his relationships with authors. I understand that independent publishers survive on trust and reputation." She paused to sip her tea. "But when I pressed him about his whereabouts yesterday evening, he got quite flustered. Claims he was making phone calls from his B&B room, but can't provide specific times or prove the calls actually happened."

That didn't sound encouraging for Marcus. "He does seem genuinely worried about his business, though. From what I've observed this weekend, his whole identity is wrapped up in being the publisher who takes risks on important work. I'm sure with a little time he'll come up with a few names to support his alibi."

"Worried enough to kill for it? That's what I need to determine." DI Drake turned to face me more directly, clearly valuing my insights. "What about Angela Victor? She was leading the workshop where Gary was finally ejected."

"Angela's a respected domestic fiction author," I said, thinking about her obvious distress after the confrontation. "Being associated with a disruptive incident like that would definitely damage her standing as a workshop leader. Teaching and workshops are becoming increasingly important income sources for mid-list authors. But honestly, she seemed more embarrassed and frustrated than murderous about Gary's behavior."

"That matches my impression," DI Drake agreed, making a note in her small notebook. "Her story checks out completely. Several participants confirmed she left the workshop area with them after ejecting Gary, and she was seen chatting with other authors at the tea shop until nearly six o'clock. Multiple witnesses, solid timeline."

Hardy had finished his seaweed investigation and trotted back to us, settling at my feet with a contented sigh while keeping one eye on the harbor gulls. Austen had positioned herself under the bench in retreat from the seagull war.

"Which brings us to the last people on my current suspect list, Diana Hartwell and her assistant," DI Drake continued.

"Diana handled Gary's disruptions very professionally," I said, "but he really did attack her credibility as both a writer and instructor. That kind of public humiliation could genuinely affect her workshop bookings and speaking engagements. Like everyone in that field she needs to protect her reputation for running smooth, educational sessions. It's part of her brand."

"The assistant is actually more interesting to me," DI Drake said, her expression growing thoughtful. "Priya Patel was quite defensive about her employer during our interview, almost aggressive in defending Diana's professional standing. She kept emphasizing how unfair Gary's attacks were, how much damage he could have done to Diana's career."

That was concerning. "Priya does seem very protective of Diana. More than just normal professional loyalty?"

"Exactly what I thought. Protective enough to act on her behalf, perhaps? Young assistants have been known to take matters into their own hands to defend employers they admire." DI Drake paused, watching a seagull attempt to steal someone's sandwich near the poetry area. "She also admits to being near Oliver's shop around five o'clock, collecting feedback forms from various workshop locations. Says it was part of her duties, but it puts her in the right place at the right time."

"Though Diana herself has a solid alibi, I assume?"

"Rock solid. She was signing books at her table until well after six, with a steady stream of fans and plenty of witnesses. Whatever happened to Gary, Diana was definitely occupied elsewhere." DI Drake finished her tea and set the cup carefully on the bench beside her.

"What about Oliver? Any word on where he might have gone?"

"That's what worries me most about this whole situation," DI Drake admitted, her professional composure slipping slightly. "Oliver Blackthorn seems to have vanished completely. His car hasn't been spotted anywhere, his phone goes straight to voicemail, and none of his neighbors have seen him since Saturday afternoon. Even his shop assistant doesn't know where he is."

"So, either he's our killer and he's run," I said, voicing what we were both thinking.

"Or he's another victim," DI Drake finished grimly. "Assumptions are dangerous in an official investigation. His neighbor checked on the house when we asked, said everything looked normal from the outside, no signs of disturbance. But the complete disappearance is still troubling."

She pulled out her notebook and flipped through several pages. "What I really need from you is context about the publishing world. In your experience, which of these professional threats would be serious enough to justify murder? I understand the business implications, but I need to grasp the emotional stakes."

I considered each suspect carefully, aware that my analysis might influence how the investigation proceeded. "Sarah's agency credibility is literally her livelihood—lose that and she loses everything. Authors, publishers, her entire professional network. It would be starting over from scratch in a business built on relationships and reputation."

"And Marcus?"

"Marcus will be operating on incredibly thin margins. Independent publishing is a labor of love that barely pays the bills under the best circumstances. Losing author trust could genuinely bankrupt him and destroy his life's work in the process. His press is his legacy."

"What about Diana? Not professionally, personally," DI Drake asked, leaning forward with obvious interest. "Which of these people seemed emotionally invested enough to act violently?"

I hadn't considered personal motives until now. "That's harder to judge," I admitted. "Priya seems the most emotionally invested but it was all about protecting Diana. The others seemed more frustrated or worried than truly enraged. I'm sorry I don't know any of the participants on that level."

DI Drake nodded slowly, clearly processing my observations. "My instinct says this wasn't a crime of passion, though. The killer used a letter opener, they had to get close, had to be someone Gary would turn his back on or someone he trusted enough to let approach without suspicion."

"Do you think Oliver let Gary into the shop for some kind of private meeting?"

"That's the most likely scenario. Oliver had keys, obviously, and Gary might have wanted to continue their argument from the workshop in private. But if Oliver killed Gary, where is he hiding? And if someone else killed Gary in Oliver's shop, what happened to Oliver?" DI Drake stood and brushed a few crumbs from her jacket, apparently she'd been stress-eating Elspeth's biscuits during interviews. "I'm going to need to dig much deeper into everyone's movements yesterday evening. And I may need to ask for your help again; you understand these people and their world in ways I simply don't."

As she prepared to head back toward the village hall, I found myself thinking about her key observation. Someone Gary trusted enough to let approach. Someone who could get close with a letter opener without Gary becoming suspicious or defensive.

The problem was, Gary's paranoia meant he didn't seem to trust anyone at the fair. He'd spent the entire weekend treating every professional as a potential enemy, every piece of advice as attempted suppression. Which suggested either the killer had caught him completely off guard, or Gary had been lured into a false sense of security by someone he thought was genuinely on his side.

Both dogs had remained unusually quiet during my conversation with DI Drake, as if they sensed the gravity of what we were discussing. Now they pressed closer to me, apparently sharing my growing unease about the investigation's direction. Hardy's tail had stopped its usual cheerful wagging, and he kept glancing between DI Drake and me with worried eyes, while Austen sat perfectly still, her ears swiveling at every sound from the fair behind us.

Because if DI Drake was right about this being a calculated killing rather than a crime of passion, then we were dealing with someone far more dangerous than a frustrated author or publisher seeking revenge for professional embarrassment.

We were dealing with someone who had planned Gary's death carefully, executed it efficiently, and was smart enough to avoid detection while continuing to participate normally in our pleasant village book fair.

The thought sent a chill through me despite the warm afternoon sunshine.

14

The afternoon brought a blessed lull in the drama, with fairgoers settling into the comfortable rhythm of browsing books and chatting about everything except murder. I was arranging the mystery display when Beau wandered over, looking rather like a professor who'd just discovered something fascinating in the library archives.

"Ginny, you'll find this interesting," he said, patting a manila folder. "Though I'm afraid we'll need somewhere to spread things out properly."

"The back office?" I suggested. "Fair warning, it's about the size of a broom cupboard, but it has a desk."

"Perfect."

The office was indeed cramped, with barely enough room for two chairs and a desk that had seen better decades. Hardy immediately claimed the patch of sunlight by the small window, while Austen settled by the door with the air of a secretary ready to take notes.

Beau opened his folder and began arranging pages across the desk. "DI Drake asked me to look at Gary's manuscript. The one scattered around the crime scene. I think I've found something rather intriguing."

"More conspiracy theories?" I asked, settling into the rickety chair.

"Actually, the opposite." Beau pointed to one section of pages. "Look at this opening chapter. The writing is quite good, solid character development, believable dialogue, proper pacing. It reads like someone who actually knows what they're doing."

I examined the pages. "That doesn't sound like the Gary we met."

"Exactly. But then you get to these sections—" He indicated pages covered in Gary's distinctive handwriting. "Suddenly it's all wooden dialogue and characters delivering speeches about government corruption. It's like watching someone take a perfectly decent thriller and systematically ruin it."

"Maybe he had an off day?"

"For two-thirds of the manuscript?" Beau shook his head. "In my experience, authors have consistent voices. This feels like watching Dr. Jekyll turn into Mr. Hyde, if Mr. Hyde was particularly obsessed with institutional conspiracy."

Freya appeared in the doorway with two steaming mugs. "Thought you might need tea," she said, then paused at our serious expressions. "Please tell me you've found something that makes sense of this whole mess."

"We might have," I said, accepting the tea gratefully. "Beau thinks Gary's manuscript shows signs of multiple authors."

"You mean like a collaboration?" Freya squeezed into the remaining space, which meant Hardy had to relocate to under the desk, where he promptly began investigating everyone's shoes.

"More like vandalism," Beau replied. "The original sections are professionally written. Gary's additions read like someone took a perfectly good book and decided to 'improve' it by adding lengthy explanations of why the postal service is probably controlled by shadow government."

"That does sound like Gary," Freya admitted. "During his workshop meltdown, he kept going on about how he'd 'enhanced' the original to expose real truth. Made it sound like he was editing something that already existed."

Beau looked up with interest. "Enhanced the original?"

"That's what he said. And here's the odd bit, he kept referring to 'the original' like it was something separate from his work." Freya settled more comfortably into her cramped space. "Plus, now that I think about it, look at the papers. The good writing is all typed, but Gary's terrible additions are handwritten."

"So he was working from someone else's typed manuscript," I mused, while Austen watched this revelation with what I could swear was approval.

"Could be lots of explanations," Beau said thoughtfully. "Writing partner, hired help, maybe he found an old manuscript at a car boot sale."

"Or maybe," Freya said with a knowing look, "he just nicked it. People steal papers and essays all the time, download them from writing forums, claim someone else's work as their own. Happens constantly."

We sat in contemplative silence for a moment, listening to the cheerful sounds of the fair continuing outside and Hardy's determined investigation of Beau's particularly interesting shoe.

"But how could we figure out who wrote the original?" Freya asked. "It's not like we can ask Gary where he got it."

"Actually," Beau said, brightening, "there might be ways. If someone submitted this to an online critique group, or shared it in a writing workshop, or entered it in contests. That sort of thing leaves digital footprints."

"Well, that doesn't narrow things down much," I pointed out. "I mean, Oliver's hardly the type to write a political thriller. The most creative thing he's ever written is probably a catalog for an auction. But Sarah deals with manuscripts constantly, Marcus publishes them, even Diana could have written something years ago that Gary somehow got hold of."

"True," Freya said, looking slightly deflated. "So we've gone from 'who wanted to kill Gary for being annoying' to 'who wanted to kill Gary for being annoying AND stealing their work.' Not exactly progress."

"Oh, I don't know," Beau said with a slight smile, gathering up the papers. "At least now we understand why someone might have been driven to use a letter opener. Watching Gary butcher your work and take credit for it? That would send any writer right round the bend."

As Beau headed off to share his discovery with DI Drake, I couldn't help thinking that somewhere among our pleasant gathering of book lovers was someone nursing a very personal grievance.

15

The Tidehaven Cove Literary Fair had officially concluded at five o'clock, and despite everything that had happened, it had been a surprising success. Browsers had bought books, authors had connected with readers, and the village had proven it could host a proper literary gathering. Tomorrow, volunteers would arrive to dismantle the stalls and pack away the bunting, and over the next few days I'd receive reports from vendors and presenters about sales and feedback. But for now, the green was peaceful, and I was finally allowing myself to feel cautiously proud of what we'd accomplished.

I was washing up the dinner dishes when a knock at the door sent both dogs into their usual greeting committee routine, though their tails suggested this was someone they knew and approved of.

Elliot stood on my doorstep with a bottle of wine and a slightly sheepish expression.

"I hope I'm not intruding," he said. "I thought you might need some company after the weekend you've had. And I brought something that might help us unwind."

"That's very thoughtful," I replied, stepping aside to let him in. "Though I should warn you, Beau's here too. We've been going over some of the manuscript evidence."

"Ah." Elliot's smile flickered only slightly. "Well, perhaps I can contribute something useful for once."

We settled in the living room, where Beau had commandeered my coffee table and covered it with photo-copied pages from Gary's manuscript. Hardy had claimed his usual spot on the hearth rug, while Austen perched on the window seat, keeping watch over the evening's activities.

"Any progress?" Elliot asked, pouring wine for all of us.

"Some," Beau said, looking up from his papers. "I've been comparing the original sections with Gary's additions, and the quality difference is even more striking than I initially thought."

"How so?"

Beau held up two pages side by side. "This chapter opening has genuine tension and characters who behave like actual human beings. It reads like someone with real publishing experience wrote it."

He flipped to another section. "But then Gary added this twenty-page conspiracy rant about pharmaceutical compa-nies controlling veterinary medicine to suppress natural healing methods that threaten their profits."

Elliot nearly choked on his wine. "He wrote what?"

"Apparently the villain's evil plan involves manipulating pet owners through their veterinarians to create depen-dency on expensive treatments instead of promoting holistic animal care." Beau's expression was perfectly serious. "There's a particularly detailed section about how flea treat-ments are actually mind-control devices."

"Good God," Elliot said weakly. "No wonder people

thought he was completely mad. The man's paranoia covers a very broad range."

"The tragic thing is," Beau continued, "the original story was actually rather good. A solid political thriller about corruption in local government, believable characters, decent pacing. It needed work, probably a thorough edit and some structural revisions, but someone who knew what they were doing wrote that foundation."

"And then Gary systematically destroyed it," I added, settling back into my favorite chair with my wine.

"More than destroyed it," Beau said, shuffling through more pages. "He turned it into a paranoid manifesto. Every time the original author had a character make a reasonable observation about politics or society, Gary added five pages explaining how that observation was actually evidence of vast conspiracy."

Elliot leaned forward thoughtfully. "It feels like the world is full of delusions these days. People who can't just accept that sometimes things are what they appear to be—everything has to be part of some vast conspiracy."

"Exactly," Beau agreed. "Gary couldn't just let a good thriller be a good thriller. He had to make it prove his theories about everything wrong with the world."

"Have you found any clues about who might have written the original?" I asked.

Beau held up a few pages covered in his notes. "Actually, yes. The writing style suggests someone familiar with British political systems and local government structures. There are references to specific parliamentary procedures, local council dynamics, even some insider knowledge about how planning permissions work in small communities."

"That could be anyone," Elliot pointed out. "Half the village has dealt with planning permissions at some point."

"True, but there's more. The writing shows real under-standing of character relationships and emotional dynam-ics. Even in what's left, you can see the author has a genuine feel for how people interact, how attraction develops, how tension builds between characters." Beau paused. "This wasn't written by someone who just dabbles in writing as a hobby. Someone with real talent for interpersonal dynamics wrote this."

The implications hung in the air. We all knew several people at the fair who fit that description - though I realized that with the fair officially over, DI Drake couldn't reason-ably hold all her suspects in the village much longer. Most of the visiting authors would be heading home tomorrow, though I'd noticed Colin Mitchell was still around, appar-ently in no hurry to leave. And Oliver remained mysteri-ously absent, which was becoming more troubling by the hour.

"The question is," I said slowly, "how did Gary get hold of it?"

"I've been thinking about that," Beau said. "Based on the manuscript format and the way it's structured, I suspect it was shared in an online critique group. There are comments in the margins that look like feedback from other writers, suggestions about pacing, character development, that sort of thing. Some of the pages even look like they were the original submission. Gary didn't even bother to make clean copies before adding his conspiracy theories."

"So Gary was part of an online writing group?" Elliot asked.

"Probably several. Writers join these groups to get feed-back on their work, share chapters, help each other improve." Beau gathered up some of the pages. "But they're also perfect hunting grounds for plagiarists. Someone posts a chapter for critique, and another member downloads it and disappears."

"That's terrible," I said. "These people are trying to help each other."

"Most are genuine," Beau agreed. "But there are always a few predators looking for material they can steal. Gary probably joined multiple groups, downloaded anything that looked promising, and vanished before anyone noticed."

Elliot refilled our wine glasses thoughtfully. "So somewhere out there is a writer who posted their work for feedback, probably got some encouraging responses, and then watched in horror as Gary butchered it and tried to get it published under his name."

"And who finally decided they'd had enough," I finished grimly.

We sat in contemplative silence, listening to the evening sounds from the village and the occasional contented sigh from Hardy, who had clearly decided this was an acceptable way to spend a Sunday evening.

"The sad part," Beau said eventually, "is that the original manuscript had real potential. A bit of polishing and the author would have seen multiple bids from publishers. Instead, Gary turned it into an unmitigated mess and spent all this time getting rejected while insisting the problem was conspiracy rather than quality."

"Do you think he actually believed his version was better?" Elliot asked.

"I think he believed his version was more important," Beau replied. "Gary wasn't interested in writing fiction. He wanted to expose what he saw as truth. He probably convinced himself that entertainment value was less important than educational content."

"Even if the educational content was complete nonsense," I added.

"Especially if it was complete nonsense. In Gary's mind, the more people dismissed his theories, the more it proved how dangerous his revelations were."

As the evening wound down and Elliot prepared to leave, I found myself wondering about the original author of that manuscript. Someone who'd put real effort into crafting a solid political thriller, only to have it stolen and systematically ruined by Gary's conspiracy theories.

16

M onday morning brought a blessed return to normalcy, or at least as close to normal as one could expect after hosting a literary fair that ended with a murder. I unlocked Hampton Books early, grateful for the familiar routine of checking inventory and straightening displays after the weekend's chaos.

Both dogs seemed relieved to be back in their territory, with Hardy immediately claiming his favorite spot by the front window while Austen settled near the register.

"Right then," I said to them, "let's see what's left of our stock after three days of determined book browsers."

I was pleased to discover that we'd sold nearly everything from the local authors display and made a significant dent in the mystery section. Even the poetry books, usually our slowest movers, had found new homes. Whatever else had happened this weekend, people had definitely been buying books.

I was restocking the local history section when DI Drake appeared at the front door, looking thoroughly exhausted.

"Ms. Hampton," she said, stepping inside with obvious

relief. "I hope you don't mind me dropping by, but I could use a proper cup of tea and a friendly face."

"Of course. Tea's always on." I led her toward the small seating area near the fiction section, where Malcolm kept a proper tea service for serious browsers. "You look exhausted."

"Three hours of sleep and more questions than answers," DI Drake admitted, settling into the comfortable reading chair. Both dogs immediately took up supervisory positions nearby, with Hardy offering his most sympathetic expression while Austen seemed more interested in the biscuits DI Drake might have with her tea.

I busied myself with the tea, finding comfort in the familiar ritual of warming the pot and measuring leaves. "Any word on Oliver?"

"That's partly why I'm here." DI Drake accepted her cup with a grateful sigh. "We've been searching for him since Saturday evening, but he's simply vanished. Car, phone, credit cards—nothing."

Inhaling the steam from my tea cup provided a moment to collect my thoughts. Despite Oliver's persistent campaign to buy the bookshop, and his occasionally patronizing lectures about village propriety, I found myself genuinely worried about him. During the fair, he'd been surprisingly helpful, lending his space for workshops, enduring Gary's disruptions with remarkable patience, even helping elderly customers carry their book purchases to their cars.

"Do you think something's happened to him?" I asked.

"That's what I can't work out. Either Oliver's our killer and he's scarpered, or someone else killed Gary and Oliver's..." She paused, sipping her tea. "Well, let's hope he's just lying low somewhere until things calm down."

"That would be like him, actually," I said, thinking it

through. "Oliver's not violent, but he's definitely cautious. If he saw something that frightened him, he'd protect himself first and worry about being a good citizen later."

The shop bell chimed, and Joyce Greywall from the post office peeked in. "Oh, I'm sorry. I didn't realize you were busy."

"Not at all," I called. "Come in! The new gardening books arrived yesterday if you're interested."

Joyce practically glowed with excitement. "Oh wonderful! My husband will be so pleased." She bustled toward the gardening section, then paused. "Terrible business about that poor man, though. My Albert said the whole village is talking about it."

"I imagine they are," DI Drake said diplomatically.

"Mind you," Joyce continued, apparently deciding that a detective inspector was an excellent audience, "we all saw this coming. That Gary fellow was trouble from the moment he arrived. Poor Elspeth from the tea shop said he lectured her about the sugar industry being a government conspiracy to control people's minds."

I stared at her. "He what?"

"Oh yes. Apparently white sugar is designed to make people docile while brown sugar causes revolutionary thinking, which is why it costs more." Joyce selected three gardening books with obvious satisfaction. "Elspeth was quite put out. She's been serving the same choices of sugar for thirty years without a single revolutionary incident."

After Joyce left, clutching her gardening books and clearly planning to share this conversation with the rest of the village, DI Drake and I exchanged looks.

"Well," she said finally, "that explains why Gary never got a second cup of tea anywhere."

"Poor Elspeth. She takes her hospitality very seriously." I refilled our cups, enjoying the brief moment of levity.

A familiar grey blur appeared in the doorway, Captain, the one-eyed village cat who'd made himself at home in the shop. He surveyed the scene with his usual regal disdain, gave both dogs a withering look that clearly communicated his opinion of their lack of dignity, then stalked over to the sunny patch near the poetry section and settled down for a nap.

"I see your other shop assistant has returned," DI Drake observed with amusement.

"He's been avoiding the crowds all weekend. Too much chaos for his refined sensibilities." I watched as Captain arranged himself in the sunny spot with obvious satisfaction. "You mentioned needing a friendly face. What can I do to help?"

"I've been going through everyone's statements, and there are some puzzling inconsistencies. Your friend Mr. Morrison's manuscript analysis has opened up entirely new possibilities, but I'm struggling to make sense of the details."

"The plagiarism theory?"

"Exactly. If Gary stole someone else's work, then we're looking at a completely different set of motives." DI Drake pulled out a small notebook, though she kept it closed for now. "The problem is, nearly everyone at your fair could have written fiction at some point."

"That's true. Sarah works with manuscripts professionally, Marcus publishes them, Diana writes bestsellers. Even some of our workshop participants mentioned they were aspiring novelists."

"And according to Mr. Morrison, whoever wrote that original manuscript has real talent for emotional relationships and character development."

I thought about the authors I'd met over the weekend. Colin Mitchell immediately came to mind. His Scarlett Fox romances were known for their well-developed relationships and emotional depth. But then again, so were Diana's thrillers, and Angela's domestic fiction certainly dealt with complex relationships.

Hardy suddenly perked up and trotted over to the window, tail wagging. Following his gaze, I saw Freya approaching with what appeared to be a box of pastries from the bakery.

"Reinforcements," I announced as she entered.

"I thought you might need sustenance," Freya said, opening the box to reveal an assortment of fresh scones and jam tarts. "Plus, I have gossip that might interest DI Drake."

"Oh?" DI Drake accepted a scone with obvious pleasure.

"Well, I was helping with the fair cleanup this morning, and several people mentioned seeing strange things Saturday evening around the time of the murder." Freya settled into a chair with her own pastry. "Nothing definitive, but interesting."

"What kind of things?"

"Mrs. Patterson from the flower shop swears she saw someone with dark hair near Oliver's shop around five-thirty. But then Mr. Davies from the pub said he noticed a tall person in a dark jacket in that same area about the same time. And old Mrs. Whitmore insists she saw a woman hurrying away from that direction just before six."

DI Drake made notes while juggling her scone. "Different descriptions of different people, or the same person seen by people with varying observation skills?"

"That's the question, isn't it?" Freya said cheerfully. "Though knowing our village, it's probably a bit of both.

Mrs. Whitmore's eyesight isn't what it was, and Mr. Davies had been sampling his own merchandise."

"What I find odd," I said, "is that Gary was seen being agitated around five o'clock, but then no one spotted him between five-thirty and when we found the body. That's not like Gary. He was usually too worked up to stay hidden."

"Unless he was with someone he trusted," DI Drake pointed out. "Someone who could calm him down or convince him to go somewhere private."

The implication hung in the air, made more comfortable by the warm shop atmosphere and the dogs' peaceful presence. Even discussing murder felt less ominous with tea and pastries and the familiar sounds of village life continuing outside.

"What can I do?" I hoped she had a clear task for me. I couldn't spend much more time on ifs and perhaps.

"Keep your eyes and ears open. You both understand these people and their connections better than I do." DI Drake finished her scone and gathered her notes. "And if anyone seems unusually interested in the investigation's progress, let me know. Sometimes killers can't resist checking on their own handiwork."

After DI Drake left, I found myself hoping Oliver was safe somewhere, completely unaware that half the Devon police force was looking for him. Whatever had happened to make him disappear so suddenly, I hoped it was something mundane rather than sinister.

17

I was cataloguing the morning's book deliveries on Tuesday when Beau appeared with his laptop, looking slightly bleary-eyed from what had obviously been a long night of digital detective work.

"Ginny, you need to see this," he said, settling at the small table near the poetry section. "I've been digging into Gary's online activities, and I found something rather extraordinary."

Both dogs wandered over to investigate, with Hardy immediately settling at Beau's feet while Austen sniffed around the chair legs before plopping down with a contented sigh.

"Don't tell me; more conspiracy theories about publishing cabals?" I asked, pulling up a chair beside him.

"Actually, something much more useful. I found traces of how Gary acquired his manuscript." Beau opened his laptop and scrolled through what appeared to be forum posts. "He wasn't as clever about covering his tracks as he thought."

The screen showed a writers' forum called "Aspiring Authors Network," with Gary's username "TruthSeeker47" prominently displayed across several discussion threads.

"What did you find?"

"Well, most of Gary's posts are exactly what you'd expect," Beau said, clicking through several screens. "Look at this thread about rejection letters."

He pointed to a post where Gary had written: "Another so-called 'agent' has rejected my manuscript exposing governmental corruption. Sarah Pemberton Literary Associates claims my work 'lacks commercial viability'. Obvious code for 'too dangerous for mainstream consumption.' The establishment fears truth-tellers!"

"That's definitely Gary," I said, recognizing the pompous tone immediately.

"But look at the responses," Beau continued, scrolling down. A user called "BookLover2019" had replied: "Maybe try focusing on story and characters instead of political rants? Just a thought."

Gary's response was immediate and lengthy: "Story and characters are distractions designed to make readers compliant. My enhanced political thriller serves the greater good by exposing corruption that commercial fiction deliberately obscures."

"Enhanced political thriller," I noted. "He's already talking about improving someone else's work."

"Gets better. Look at this thread from six months later." Beau clicked to another discussion about critique groups. "Someone asked for recommendations about sharing work online, and Gary posted this helpful response."

The post read: "Online critique groups are goldmines for superior base material requiring proper enhancement.

Original authors often lack courage to pursue genuine revolutionary potential. I have successfully elevated romantic drivel into meaningful political commentary."

I stared at the screen. "He's basically advertising his theft method."

"And someone called him on it. Look at this reply from 'WriterGirl23': 'Mate, if you're going to enhance someone else's work, at least give them credit. That's called plagiarism where I come from.'"

Gary's response was a masterpiece of self-justification: "Credit is irrelevant when dealing with truth suppression. Intellectual property laws exist to protect establishment interests, not genuine literary revolution. I have transformed what is basically romantic fiction masquerading as thriller into essential democratic resistance literature."

Freya appeared with the tea tray, took one look at our serious expressions, and set everything down with extra care. "Please tell me you've found something that makes sense of this whole mess."

"We've found Gary's confession to literary theft," I explained. "He's been stealing manuscripts and 'enhancing' them with his conspiracy theories."

"Enhanced," Freya said, settling into a chair with obvious interest. "That sounds delightfully awful."

Beau scrolled to another thread where Gary had posted seeking feedback on his "completed manuscript." The post was typically grandiose: "My political enhancement of commercial fiction demonstrates how romantic manipulation can be purified into genuine social commentary. Publishers fear this synthesis of entertainment and truth-telling."

A user called "StorySeeker" had responded: "Could you

share a sample? I'd be interested to see how you've blended the genres."

Gary's reply was illuminating: "The original author wasted excellent material on emotional manipulation typical of female commercial writers. I have removed superfluous romantic scenes and elevated the political content to expose real ingrained corruption."

"Female commercial writers," I read aloud. "He's not just a thief, he's a sexist thief."

"Look at this response," Beau said, pointing to another reply. "Someone called 'PlotTwister' wrote: 'So you took someone else's romance novel and rewrote it as political fiction? That's not blending genres, that's vandalism.'"

Gary's defensive response filled half the screen: "Vandalism is what publishers do to authentic political literature! They demand 'character development' and 'emotional arcs' to distract readers from institutional malfeasance. My enhancement process removes commercial contamination and focuses on essential truth-telling. The romance elements were deliberate misdirection designed to make readers compliant!"

"Good lord," Freya said, reading over my shoulder. "He really believed he was improving people's work."

"There's more," Beau said, opening another thread. "This one's from about a year ago, in a discussion about online critique groups."

Gary had posted: "I recommend the Aspiring Authors Network for acquiring source material. Writers frequently post complete manuscripts seeking feedback. Most lack the vision to pursue genuine political revelation, making their work ideal for revolutionary enhancement."

The responses to this post were uniformly horrified.

"BookBinder47" had written: "Are you seriously suggesting people should steal manuscripts from critique groups?"

"LiteraryLass" added: "This is exactly why some writers are afraid to share their work online. Predators like this ruin it for everyone."

Gary's response was unrepentant: "Sharing work publicly implies consent for improvement by superior political vision. Intellectual property protection serves establishment interests."

"He's completely shameless," I observed.

"The best part," Beau said, "is this thread from three months ago where he actually describes the theft." He clicked to show a discussion about manuscript revision.

Gary had written: "I recently completed enhancement of a romance writer's political thriller. The original author showed promise but wasted it on commercial romantic subplot. My systematic removal of emotional manipulation and addition of genuine conspiracy exposition has transformed it into essential democratic literature."

A user called "CharacterFirst" had responded: "Did you get permission from the original author? Because what you're describing sounds like plagiarism."

Gary's reply was typical: "Permission is irrelevant when serving the greater good of political awakening. The original author contaminated solid thriller material with romantic distraction. My enhancement serves democracy by exposing real corruption instead of promoting emotional compliance."

"Romance writers promoting emotional compliance," Freya said with a snort. "Because falling in love is clearly a government plot."

"Oh, it gets worse," Beau said, scrolling further. "Look at this response from someone called 'TrueRomance': 'As a romance writer, I find your attitude offensive and your theft illegal. Romance novels don't promote compliance. They promote hope, healing, and human connection. Maybe if you understood actual human emotions, your political fiction wouldn't be such rubbish.'"

Gary's response was a three-paragraph rant about how romance fiction was designed to "pacify revolutionary instincts through emotional manipulation," but the damage was clearly done. Several other forum members had piled on, calling him everything from "literary parasite" to "delusional narcissist."

"No wonder he stopped posting on that forum," I said.

"But not before leaving us a clear trail of evidence," Beau said, closing the laptop with satisfaction. "We know he stole a political thriller from a romance writer, we know he butchered it with conspiracy theories, and we know he was completely unrepentant about the theft."

"The question is," Freya said thoughtfully, "which romance writer?"

"Well, that narrows it down," I said with gentle irony. "Only about half the authors at our fair write romance in some form or another."

Freya nearly choked on her tea with sudden laughter. "You don't suppose Oliver could be a closet romance writer, do you?"

The image was so absurd that I couldn't help laughing. "Oliver? Writing romance? The man who thinks public displays of affection are unseemly?"

"Well, you never know," Freya said, clearly enjoying the idea. "Maybe that's why he's disappeared. He's mortified that his secret passion for writing bodice-rippers might be exposed."

"The Antique Dealer's Forbidden Love," I suggested,

getting into the spirit. "'She came for a Georgian tea service, but found something far more valuable...'"

"His expertise in period furniture was nothing compared to his knowledge of a lady's desires," Beau added with perfect seriousness, making us dissolve into giggles.

"Oh dear," Freya gasped, wiping her eyes. "Can you imagine the titles? Passion Among the Porcelain? The Clockmaker's Secret Romance? Love in the Time of Chippendale?"

Even Captain seemed amused by our laughter, opening one eye from his sunny spot to give us a look that clearly suggested we were disturbing important feline business.

"Seduced by Antiques," I continued, unable to stop myself. "The Mysterious Case of the Amorous Armoire."

"Pride and Porcelain," Freya added. "Sense and Sensual-Tea-Sets."

"In all seriousness though," I said, trying to regain some composure, "we do have several romance authors who extended their stays after the fair."

"That's right," Freya agreed, still giggling slightly. "Colin Mitchell is still at the B&B, and that workshop participant Jenny mentioned she was staying an extra few days for a holiday. Even some of the other authors talked about exploring Devon while they were here."

"So we're back to having plenty of suspects," Beau said, reopening his laptop. "Though at least now we know what we're looking for. A romance writer who also had the knowledge and skill to craft a solid political thriller."

"And someone who was naive enough to trust their work to an online critique group where Gary could steal it," I added.

"So now what?" Freya said thoughtfully. "Do we wait for

DI Drake to sort this out officially, or do we try to figure out who the real author is ourselves?"

"I think we should definitely share what we've found with DI Drake," I said. "But I have to admit, I'm curious to know which of our pleasant weekend guests has been harboring a secret worth killing for."

18

I was totaling the weekend's sales when Colin Mitchell appeared at Hampton Books. He stood at the front door, looking a bit less polished than during his book signings. His usually neat appearance was slightly rumpled, and both dogs lifted their heads with interest when he entered.

"Ms. Hampton," he said, stepping inside with what seemed like casual friendliness. "I hope you don't mind me dropping by. I wanted to thank you for such a wonderful fair before I head back to London."

"Of course not," I replied, though something about his manner seemed different. Hardy wandered over to investigate while Austen watched from her spot by the register. "I'm glad you enjoyed it, despite... everything that happened."

"Yes, terrible business about Gary." Colin's voice carried the right note of regret, though his hands were restless, fidgeting with the strap of his messenger bag. "Though I have to say, I'm not entirely surprised someone finally lost patience with him. The man was rather difficult."

There was something about Colin this morning that felt different from the relaxed author I'd met during the fair. He kept glancing toward the windows, and his usual easy smile seemed to require more effort.

"The police have been quite thorough," I said carefully, watching his reaction.

"Oh yes, I had another chat with DI Drake yesterday evening. Very professional woman." Colin moved closer to the fiction section, running his fingers along the book spines. "She asked some rather pointed questions about Gary's manuscript claims. Apparently someone's been suggesting his work might not have been entirely his own."

"Really?" I kept my voice neutral, though my pulse quickened.

"Mmm. Something about plagiarism, though I can't imagine where that idea came from." Colin pulled a book from the shelf and flipped through it absently. "People do love to complicate things, don't they? Sometimes the simplest explanation is the right one."

"Which would be?"

"That Gary was exactly what he appeared, a rather delusional fellow who made enemies wherever he went." Colin replaced the book and turned to face me. "Take Oliver Blackthorn, for instance. Still missing, I hear? Rather concerning."

The way he said it made me pay closer attention. There was something almost rehearsed in his tone, as if he'd been thinking for a long time about this conversation.

"The police are still looking for him," I said.

"Of course they are. Though between you and me, I've encountered Oliver at a few antique fairs over the years. I collect vintage fountain pens for my writing, and he occasionally has some lovely pieces. He's always struck me as the type to cut and run when things get difficult." Colin moved to the window, peering out at the green, which had returned to its usual peaceful state. "Bit of a temper, you know. Probably acted in anger and then panicked."

"You sound rather certain about that," I observed.

"Well, who else could it be?" Colin's laugh sounded a bit forced. "Sarah Pemberton seems far too professional to resort to violence. Marcus Webb is such a gentle soul. I can't imagine him hurting anyone. Diana Hartwell has always struck me as very controlled, very civilized. It's hard to picture any of them with a letter opener."

There was something about his systematic dismissal of the suspects that felt as rehearsed as before. I suppose it would be rude to ask if he put himself on the list.

"What about Angela Victor?" I asked, curious to see his response.

"Angela?" Colin shook his head. "She writes lovely domestic fiction. I doubt she's ever encountered real violence, let alone committed it." He paused, seeming to catch himself. "Not that I mean to disparage domestic fiction, of course. It serves an important purpose."

"Which is?"

"Comfort reading. Gentle stories for people who want to feel better about their lives." There was something in Colin's tone that suggested he didn't entirely approve. "Nothing wrong with that, but hardly the sort of thing that leads to murderous passion."

The shop bell chimed, and Freya entered with an armload of books and papers, clearly returning from collecting receipts and feedback forms from the various vendors. She paused when she saw Colin, her expression shifting from cheerful to cautious.

"Oh, hello Colin. I didn't expect to see you still in the village."

"Just saying my goodbyes," Colin replied, though I noticed his hands had tightened into fists at his sides. "Lovely fair, despite the unfortunate end."

"Mm." Freya's response was diplomatic as she set her papers on the counter. Both dogs immediately went over to greet her, tails wagging with obvious pleasure. "Any word on Oliver?"

"We were just discussing that," Colin said. "I was telling Ginny how obvious it seems that Oliver's our culprit. Who else had both motive and opportunity?"

Freya raised her eyebrows. "Obvious? I thought the police were still investigating."

"Oh, they are. But really, it's quite clear when you think about it sensibly." Colin began walking around near the windows, his restless energy becoming more apparent. "Oliver hosted the workshop where Gary was ejected. Gary embarrassed him publicly, questioned his professional credibility. Then Gary turns up dead in Oliver's shop, and Oliver conveniently disappears. It's hardly a complex puzzle."

"You seem to have given this quite a lot of thought," Freya said, her tone carefully neutral.

"Well, one can't help but wonder. It's rather like something out of a crime novel—except the plot's more straightforward than most fiction." Colin's smile seemed tight. "Real life tends to be less complicated than what we writers imagine."

"Does it?" I asked. "In my experience, real life is usually much more complex than it appears on the surface."

Something flickered in Colin's eyes, a brief moment of what might have been worry, quickly hidden. "Sometimes, perhaps. But in this case, I think we're dealing with a very human situation. Anger, embarrassment, a moment of poor judgment, and then panic. Rather predictable, really."

The way he described it was oddly detached, as if he was discussing a book plot rather than a real person's death.

"Have you finished packing?" Freya asked, clearly trying to steer the conversation elsewhere.

"Nearly. Though I'm in no particular hurry to leave Devon. Lovely countryside, and the B&B is quite comfortable." Colin glanced at his watch. "Though I suppose I should let you get back to your work. Running a bookshop must keep you both quite busy."

"It has its moments," I agreed.

Colin moved toward the door, then paused as if something had just occurred to him. "You know, I've been thinking about Gary's manuscript claims. All that nonsense about political thrillers and government conspiracy. If Gary did steal someone else's work, which seems increasingly likely, it was probably just amateur writers sharing material online. These writing forums are full of people whose work gets copied."

"Is that common?" I asked, interested in an author's perspective.

"More common than you'd think. People post chapters for feedback, someone downloads them and rewrites. Happens quite regularly." Colin's tone was matter-of-fact, but there was something careful in his posture. "Of course, most stolen work isn't worth much anyway. Real writers don't need to steal; we have our own ideas."

After Colin left, Freya and I stood quietly for a moment while both dogs gradually settled back into their usual spots.

"That was a bit odd," Freya said finally, picking up one of the books from her pile and examining its spine.

"Mm," I agreed, straightening some papers on the counter. "He seemed quite certain about Oliver being the culprit."

"Very certain. Almost like he'd been intentionally planting a seed." Freya opened the book to check for any damage from the weekend's activities. "And all that knowledge about online writing forums, I didn't realize he was so familiar with how manuscript theft works."

I nodded thoughtfully, watching Hardy stretch contentedly in his sunny spot. "Perhaps we should mention his visit to DI Drake when she stops by."

"Good idea," Freya said, adding the book to the pile of ones that needed reshelfing. "Though I'm sure she's keeping track of everyone's comings and goings anyway."

The morning light was particularly lovely streaming through the front windows, and despite everything that had happened, there was something comforting about returning to the familiar routine of organizing books and chatting with Freya about the weekend's events. Even with a murder investigation ongoing, life in Tidehaven Cove had a way of maintaining its gentle rhythm.

19

Tuesday evening found me in the bookshop after closing, surrounded by photocopied pages from Gary's manuscript and Beau's extensive notes from his online investigation. The familiar smell of old books and Malcolm's lavender furniture polish made the shop feel cozy despite the serious nature of our task. The reading lamps cast warm pools of light across our workspace, leaving the rest of the shop in comfortable shadows.

Both dogs had settled into their evening positions. Hardy sprawled across the rug near the poetry section, Austen keeping watch from the window seat. I'd given them each a dental chew from the jar Malcolm kept behind the counter, and they were contentedly gnawing away.

"I keep coming back to this," I said, holding up one of the original typed pages. "The romantic subplot that Gary tried to remove. Look at how it's written."

Beau leaned over to examine the page more closely, accidentally knocking over his tea cup—thankfully empty. "What about it?"

"The emotional dynamics are perfect. The way attraction builds between the characters, the subtle push and pull of desire and professional obligation." I traced a finger along one particularly well-crafted paragraph. "This isn't someone dabbling in romance as a subplot. This is someone who really understands how to write romantic tension."

"You're thinking of Colin," Beau said, not as a question but as confirmation of what we'd both been circling around all day.

"He's kept such a low profile," I said slowly. "Diana mentioned he was sympathetic when she vented about Gary, and Marcus said Colin agreed the whole situation was unfortunate, but he hasn't sought anyone out or tried to involve himself."

"It could be seen as classic behavior for someone trying to avoid attention," Beau observed. "Stay visible enough not to seem suspicious, but don't engage enough to be memorable."

Through the window, I could hear the village settling into its evening routine. The distant clatter of dishes from the pub kitchen, someone calling their cat in for the night. It all seemed so normal, so removed from murder and literary theft.

I shuffled through more pages, finding one of Gary's handwritten additions. "Look at this section where Gary added his conspiracy rant about publishing gatekeepers. He specifically mentions romance writers as 'promoting emotional compliance' and 'distracting from real political issues.'"

"Which would be particularly galling if you were a romance writer who'd written a political thriller," Beau said.

The shop bell chimed as Freya burst through the door slightly out of breath and carrying a paper bag from Elspeth's tea shop.

"You need to hear this," she announced without preamble, setting the bag on the counter. "But first, Elspeth insisted I bring these. Said you'd probably forgotten to eat dinner again."

The smell of fresh scones wafted from the bag, making me realize I actually had forgotten dinner. Both dogs immediately abandoned their chews, padding over to investigate this new development with hopeful tail wags. I appreciated it, but if I continued to survive on pastries I would be waddling within a week.

"What did you need to tell us?" I prompted, breaking off a piece of a cheese scone.

"I've been at the pub, and Jenny—you know, the workshop participant who's staying extra days—she was in an online critique group with Colin about eighteen months ago."

"And?" I asked, tossing small pieces of scone to each dog, who caught them with practiced ease.

"Colin posted chapters of a political thriller he was working on. Jenny says it was really good, much darker and more serious than his usual romance work. But then he suddenly deleted everything and left the group without explanation."

"When was this?" Beau asked, pulling out his laptop while absently reaching for a scone.

"Last year sometime. Spring maybe? Jenny said Colin seemed really excited about branching into a new genre, kept talking about how this book would show he could write more than just romance." Freya settled into a chair, accepting the cup of tea I poured from the pot Malcolm always left ready.

I felt the pieces clicking into place. "And then Gary stole it."

"It fits the timeline," Beau confirmed, scrolling through his notes while getting crumbs on his keyboard. "Gary's forum posts about 'enhancing' romance manuscripts start about sixteen months ago."

"But Colin never said anything," I mused. "Never confronted Gary publicly, never accused him of theft."

"Would you?" Freya asked. "Imagine being a successful romance author and having to admit that your attempt at darker fiction was not only stolen but turned into paranoid conspiracy drivel. The humiliation would be unbearable."

That rang true. Colin had built a successful career as Scarlett Fox, but I'd noticed subtle comments over the weekend suggesting he felt constrained by the genre's expectations. The stolen thriller might have been his attempt to prove himself as a "serious" writer.

Outside, the church bells chimed nine o'clock, their bronze voices carrying clearly through the quiet evening air. It was getting late, but we were too deep into our discovery to stop now.

"We need to check something," I said, moving to the shop computer. "Colin's website—his Scarlett Fox author site."

The website loaded with romantic imagery, soft focus couples, flowing script, testimonials from devoted readers about how his books had touched their hearts. But I navigated to the "About" section.

"There," I said, pointing to a seemingly innocuous line in his biography. "Before writing romance, Colin worked in local government administration for five years."

"Local government," Beau said slowly. "Just like the insider knowledge in the original manuscript."

"And look at this blog post from two years ago," I continued, clicking through the archives. "He talks about wanting to expand his writing, to tackle 'more serious themes while maintaining the emotional truth that readers expect.'"

"He practically announced he was writing a political thriller," Freya said, reading over my shoulder.

Hardy had finished hoping for more scone crumbs and settled at my feet with a contented sigh, while Austen maintained her post by the window, occasionally lifting her head at the sound of footsteps on the pavement outside. Late evening dog walkers, most likely.

"There's more," Beau said, pulling up Gary's forum posts again. "Look at this thread where someone challenges Gary about stealing. The username 'FoxWriter98' posted: 'You're a parasite feeding off real writers' work. Someone should stop you before you destroy anything else'."

"FoxWriter," I said. "As in Scarlett Fox?"

"The post was deleted almost immediately, but the quote was preserved in another user's reply." Beau's expression was grim. "Colin was watching Gary destroy his work and getting angrier."

"But why kill him now?" Freya asked. "Why not months ago when the theft first happened?"

I thought about Colin's behavior over the weekend. "Because Gary was here, in person, still pushing the manuscript as his own work. Still claiming it was brilliant, still insisting publishers were suppressing it because it was too dangerous."

"While the real author had to watch and pretend everything was fine," Beau added.

"Worse than that," I realized with sudden clarity. "Colin had to watch Gary dismiss romance writing as emotional manipulation while pushing a bastardized version of Colin's own attempt to transcend genre limitations."

We sat in silence for a moment, absorbing the implications. The shop felt very quiet, just the ticking of Malcolm's antique clock and the gentle sound of both dogs settling deeper into sleep. The scones sat forgotten on their plates, tea growing cold in our cups.

"We need to tell DI Drake," Freya said.

"We need proof first," I countered. "Right now this is all speculation based on usernames and timeline coincidences."

"What about Colin's laptop?" Beau suggested. "If he wrote the original manuscript, there might be drafts, notes, something showing his authorship."

"He's been very careful," I said, thinking about Colin's behavior. "Always pleasant, always professional, but never particularly engaged. Like he was playing a part."

"Except," Freya said suddenly, "he's still here. Most of the out-of-town authors left Sunday or Monday. Why is Colin still in Tidehaven Cove?"

That was an excellent question. "Maybe because he's waiting to see if he'll get away with it?"

"Or because he's not done yet," Beau said quietly.

We all looked at each other, the implication hanging in the air. If Colin had killed to protect his secret, who else might he consider a threat?

"Oliver," I said suddenly. "Oliver's still missing. What if Oliver saw something, knows something?"

"We need to find DI Drake now," Beau said, already reaching for his phone.

But before he could dial, we heard a sound from the back of the shop—something shifting in the storage room behind the local history section. A soft thud, like books being moved.

Both dogs were instantly alert, their relaxed contentment vanishing. Hardy's hackles rose as he got to his feet, while Austen abandoned her window post to move closer to me, both of them producing low, warning growls that I'd rarely heard from them before.

"What was that?" Freya whispered.

Another sound—definitely footsteps now, moving through the back room. Whoever it was wasn't trying to be particularly quiet. The storage room door handle turned slowly.

"Someone's been in the shop all along," I said quietly, my heart racing. "They must have hidden when we closed—"

The storage room door opened, and Colin Mitchell stepped into the shop, looking perfectly calm and carrying what appeared to be a manuscript box. He was dressed differently than during the fair, dark clothes that would blend into shadows, practical shoes that had made those purposeful footsteps.

"Hello, Ginny," he said pleasantly, though something in his eyes made both dogs move protectively closer to me, their growls deepening. "I thought I might find you here. We need to talk about Gary's manuscript. Or rather, my manuscript. I think it's time we discussed who really wrote 'Shadow of Power.'"

The letter opener in his other hand caught the light from the desk lamp, its brass surface gleaming. I recognized it immediately, it was from the antique set Malcolm kept on the rare books desk, supposedly used by Virginia Woolf though Malcolm could never prove it.

20

Me first instinct was to run. To bolt for the door and get help. But Colin stood between us and the main exit, and the back door was locked from the inside. Even if one of us could get out, that would mean leaving the others alone with him. I couldn't live with myself if Freya or Beau got hurt because I'd run for help. Better to stay together, try to keep him calm, and look for an opportunity when we could all get to safety.

"How long have you been hiding back there?" Freya's voice rose in alarm, her usual cheerfulness replaced by genuine fear. "We've been here for over an hour!"

Colin's smile was apologetic but not particularly sincere. "Since just before closing. I slipped in while Malcolm was helping that last customer with the recipe books, then waited in the storage room behind those boxes of unsold poetry anthologies." He shifted the manuscript box under his arm. "Mrs. Patterson mentioned at the tea shop that you often work late on Tuesday evenings, Ginny. Something about it being your catch-up night after the weekend. And with everything that's happened, I figured you'd be trying to piece it together."

Both dogs had positioned themselves between Colin and our little group, their growling more pronounced now. Hardy's usually cheerful demeanor had vanished entirely, while Austen looked ready to launch herself at Colin if he made any sudden moves.

"You've been listening to us this whole time?" Freya's voice was smaller now, and she unconsciously moved closer to Beau.

"Most of it," Colin admitted. "You were getting very close to the truth. I thought it was time to explain myself properly." He glanced at the manuscript box. "And I needed to retrieve this. I'd hidden it back there on Saturday afternoon, after... after I dealt with Gary. I couldn't risk it being found with his things."

The casual way he said "dealt with Gary" made my blood run cold, though the warm lamplight and lingering scent of scones created a surreal contrast to the menace in his words.

"Why don't you sit down?" I suggested, trying to keep my voice steady while mentally calculating distances to exits. "Tell us what really happened. The tea's still warm."

Colin actually laughed at that, a bitter sound that seemed wrong in our cozy bookshop. "How very British. Murder confession over tea and scones." But he did move toward the chairs, though he kept the letter opener visible. "I suppose you've worked it out by now. The manuscript, I mean."

"You wrote the original political thriller," Beau said carefully, his Southern accent more pronounced, something that happened when he was stressed. "Gary stole it from an online critique group."

"Stole it and butchered it," Colin corrected, his pleasant mask slipping to reveal genuine anger. "Do you have any idea what it's like to watch someone take your work—work you poured your soul into,—and systematically destroy it with paranoid drivel about government conspiracies?"

He set the manuscript box on the small table between us, his hand still gripping the letter opener. Through the shop window, I could see lights in the buildings across the green, people living their normal evening lives, having no idea what was happening in our bookshop.

"This is my original," Colin said, opening the box to reveal neatly typed pages. "The only clean copy I have left. I brought it with me to the fair, hoping... I don't know what I was hoping. Maybe that I could somehow reclaim it, make things right."

"You've been carrying it all weekend?" I asked, trying to keep him talking while searching for a way out of this situation.

"In my room at the B&B at first. But after Saturday, after what happened with Gary, I needed it somewhere safer. Somewhere the police wouldn't immediately search." He gestured toward the storage room. "I remembered seeing the back room when Freya gave that behind-the-scenes tour of the bookshop on Friday, showing how a proper bookshop operates, she called it."

"I spent two years on that novel," Colin continued, settling into Malcolm's favorite reading chair. "Two years researching local government corruption, crafting characters with real emotional depth, building a plot that actually made sense. It was going to be my breakout from romance, my proof that I could write 'serious' fiction."

"There's nothing unserious about romance," Freya said

with surprising firmness, apparently finding courage in defending the genre despite her fear.

"Try telling that to literary critics," Colin replied bitterly. "Try telling that to other authors who smirk when you introduce yourself as a romance writer. Try telling that to Gary, who spent the entire weekend explaining how romance novels were 'emotional manipulation designed to make readers compliant',"

Hardy had stopped growling but remained standing, ready to protect us if needed. Austen had positioned herself slightly behind him, not from fear, but in what looked like a tactical position.

"So you posted chapters to get feedback," I prompted, hoping to keep him talking while I tried to figure out how to signal for help. My phone was in my bag behind the counter, frustratingly out of reach.

"I was so proud of those chapters," Colin said, his voice taking on a dreamy quality. "The critique group loved them. Said they were fresh, compelling, that I'd successfully blended emotional authenticity with political thriller elements. For the first time, I felt like I might be taken seriously as more than just 'Scarlett Fox, romance writer.'"

He pulled out a page from his manuscript box. "Look at this—my original opening. No conspiracy theories, no paranoid ranting, just solid thriller writing with real emotional depth."

"When did you realize Gary had stolen it?" Beau asked, managing to sound genuinely interested rather than terrified.

"Sixteen months and three days ago," Colin said precisely. "It was a Tuesday. I remember because I'd just posted my weekly blog update about my writing progress. I'd noticed someone had downloaded all my chapters from the critique group, you can see the download statistics. Then a few weeks later, I saw a forum post where someone calling himself 'TruthSeeker47' was bragging about 'enhancing' a romance writer's political thriller." Colin's grip on the letter opener tightened. "I knew immediately it was my work."

The church bells chimed the half hour; nine-thirty. The sound seemed to bring Colin back to the present, and his expression hardened.

"I tried to ignore it at first. Thought maybe he'd give up when publishers rejected him. But he didn't give up. He kept submitting it, kept adding more conspiracy theories, kept making it worse." Colin stood abruptly, making both dogs tense. "And then he showed up here, at your lovely little literary fair, still pushing my manuscript as his own work."

"That must have been unbearable," I said, trying to project sympathy while calculating whether we could all make it to the door if he moved away from it.

"Friday was bad enough, listening to him rant about publishing conspiracies. But Saturday..." Colin moved toward the window, looking out at the peaceful village green. "Saturday he cornered me during lunch. Told me he'd read some of my 'commercial romance fiction' and that I had 'technical skill that could be put to better use exposing deception instead of promoting emotional compliance.'"

"He had no idea he was talking to the person he'd stolen from," Freya said quietly.

"None at all. He actually tried to recruit me to help him 'enhance' other romance manuscripts. Said together we could transform 'trivial entertainment into revolutionary literature.'" Colin turned back to face us, and I could see tears in his eyes. "He stood there with my manuscript, my work that he'd destroyed, and patronized me about my successful career."

The shop felt very quiet except for the ticking of Malcolm's clock and the soft sound of Austen's worried whine. She could sense the emotional turmoil in the room, and it was clearly distressing her.

"So you arranged to meet him Saturday evening," Beau said. It wasn't a question.

"I told him I had some thoughts about his manuscript. Suggested we meet privately in Oliver's shop. He told me Oliver gave him the key so he could retrieve something he'd left behind." Colin's voice was matter-of-fact now, as if he were describing plot points in one of his novels. "I'm sure he stole the key because that's who he was. I must say, Gary was thrilled. Thought he'd finally found an ally who understood his vision."

"And the letter opener?" I asked, glancing at the one still in his hand.

"I didn't plan that part. It was just there, on Oliver's desk. Gary was going through his butchered version of my manuscript, explaining how each conspiracy theory he'd added elevated my original work, and I just... snapped." Colin looked at the letter opener in his hand as if surprised to find it there. "One moment he was explaining how my romantic subplot was 'establishment propaganda,' and the next..."

He trailed off, but we could all fill in the blanks.

"You screamed," I said suddenly, remembering. "We heard someone scream."

"Did I? I don't remember that. I just remember running. Leaving through the back entrance and walking home as if nothing had happened. I even stopped to chat with Mrs. Patterson about her roses." He laughed again, that bitter sound. "Ten minutes after killing a man, and I was discussing the best fertilizer for English roses."

Through the window, I saw a figure approaching the shop, someone walking a dog, pausing to look at our lit windows. For a moment I hoped they might come in, but they moved on, leaving us alone with Colin and his confession.

"What now?" Freya asked in a small voice. "What are you planning to do with us?"

Colin looked genuinely surprised by the question. "I'm not some serial killer from one of Diana's thrillers. I just wanted to explain, to make someone understand why I did it. And I needed to retrieve my manuscript—the real one, not Gary's abomination."

"Then why the letter opener?" Beau asked pointedly.

Colin looked down at it again, seeming to realize how it must appear. "Habit, I suppose. Taking a weapon when confronting potential threats. Very thriller-writer of me, isn't it?" He chuckled as he set it down on the table with a soft clink. "I'm not going to hurt anyone else. I just couldn't let Gary's version of my work become the official record."

Both dogs relaxed slightly when he put the letter opener down, though they maintained their protective positions. Hardy even wagged his tail tentatively, as if hoping the situation might resolve itself peacefully.

"You need to turn yourself in," I said gently. "DI Drake will understand. Crime of passion, temporary insanity—"

"Will she understand that I spent over a year watching him destroy my work? Will a jury understand what it's like to see your attempt at serious literature turned into paranoid ranting?" Colin shook his head. "I don't think so. But I'm not running either. I just wanted one night to put my affairs in order."

He picked up his manuscript box, holding it like something precious. "This is all I have left of what the book should have been. Before Gary's 'enhancements,' before the conspiracy theories, before it all went wrong."

"Colin," I started, but he was already moving toward the door.

"I'll be at the B&B if DI Drake wants to find me. Room three, the one with the view of the harbor." He paused at the door, looking back at us with something like regret. "I really am sorry about frightening you, Freya. And Ginny, the fair really was lovely. Despite everything." He turned to Beau. "And Mr. Morrison, your analysis of the manuscript was brilliant. Perhaps you'll consider publishing my manuscript. I'll contact you."

And then he was gone, leaving us sitting in the warm lamplight with cooling tea and uneaten scones, trying to process what had just happened.

"Should we call the police now?" Freya asked, her voice shaky.

"I'm calling DI Drake directly," I said, already moving toward my bag behind the counter. "She needs to know Colin just confessed and where to find him."

As I dialed her number, I looked at the letter opener Colin had left behind, thinking about how sometimes the cozy world of books and tea could crack open to reveal something much darker underneath. Even in a place as pleasant as Tidehaven Cove, where people discussed roses after committing murder and confessed to crimes over scones.

"Drake here," came the crisp answer on the second ring.

"It's Ginny Hampton. Colin Mitchell just confessed to killing Gary. He's heading back to the B&B, room three. He says he won't run."

"Is anyone hurt? Are you safe?"

"We're fine. He's gone. But you should hurry. He said he wanted one night to put his affairs in order."

"On my way. Don't touch anything he might have left behind."

As I ended the call, I noticed my hands were shaking slightly.

The dogs seemed to sense the danger had passed, and Hardy padded over to rest his head on my knee, seeking comfort or perhaps offering it.

21

We waited in the bookshop for DI Drake to arrive, none of us quite ready to be alone yet. Freya had made fresh tea with shaking hands, apparently needing the familiar ritual to steady herself. Beau sat quietly, studying the letter opener Colin had left behind without touching it. Both dogs had settled into protective positions; Hardy pressed against my legs, Austen right beside him.

"Ten minutes," I said, checking my watch again. "She should be here any moment."

"Do you think he'll actually be there?" Freya asked, wrapping her hands around her teacup as if drawing warmth from it. "At the B&B?"

"He said he would be," Beau observed. "But he also said he wanted a night to put his affairs in order. That could mean anything."

The shop felt different at night, cozier somehow, with pools of warm light from the reading lamps and deep shadows between the shelves. The familiar smell of old books and furniture polish was comforting, even as we sat processing what had just happened. Captain, the one-eyed village cat, had appeared from wherever he spent his evenings and settled on top of the poetry section, watching us with regal indifference.

Through the window, we saw police cars approaching without sirens but with lights flashing, their blue strobes painting strange patterns across the village green. DI Drake's unmarked car pulled up directly outside the shop.

"Stay here," I said, moving toward the door. "I'll let her in."

DI Drake entered with two uniformed officers, her expression professional but concerned. She looked tired, this was her second murder investigation in our village this year. "Is everyone all right?"

"We're fine," I assured her. "Just shaken. Would you like tea? Freya just made a fresh pot."

"No time, I'm afraid." She pulled on latex gloves. "Show me exactly where he was and what he touched."

I walked her through Colin's movements—from the storage room where he'd been hiding, to Malcolm's chair where he'd sat, to the table where he'd placed his manuscript box and eventually the letter opener.

"He brought his original manuscript," I explained. "The one Gary stole before adding all his conspiracy theories. He'd hidden it in our storage room on Saturday after... after the murder."

"We'll need full statements from all of you," DI Drake said, photographing the letter opener. "But first, I need to get to the B&B." She spoke into her radio. "All units, approach the Harbour View B&B with caution. Subject has confessed but may be unstable."

Her radio crackled with static, then Constable Trewin's voice came through: "Ma'am, at the B&B now. Mrs. Henley says Mr. Mitchell is in room three. Light's on, classical music playing."

"Good. We'll be there in five minutes. Approach but do not engage until I arrive."

She turned back to us. "I'll send someone to take your statements. Please stay here until they arrive."

But just as she reached the door, her radio crackled again. "Ma'am, subject's on the move. Just saw him leave through the back garden. He's heading toward the harbor path."

DI Drake's expression darkened. "All units converge on the harbor. Set up a perimeter." She looked back at us. "Lock the door after me. Do not leave until an officer comes for your statements."

After she left, we sat in stunned silence for a moment. Freya poured more tea with shaking hands, the everyday ritual helping to ground us. Even Captain seemed to sense the tension, abandoning his perch to wind around Freya's legs comfortingly.

"He's running," Freya said quietly. "After all that calm confession, he's actually running."

"Can't blame him, really," Beau said. "The reality of prison must have hit once he left here."

Through the window, we could see more police cars racing past, all heading toward the harbor. The village was waking up, lights appearing in windows, curtains twitching as residents peered out to see what was happening.

A young detective constable arrived within twenty minutes, looking harried. "I'm DC Morrison. I need to take brief statements, just the essential facts about Mr. Mitchell's confession. DI Drake wants full statements tomorrow."

We went through the basics quickly: Colin's appearance, his confession about the manuscript theft, his admission of killing Gary. The constable was professional but clearly eager to rejoin the manhunt.

"Right, that's enough for now," he said, closing his notebook. "You should all go home and lock your doors. We'll be in touch tomorrow for full statements."

"Is it safe?" Freya asked. "With Colin out there?"

"We'll have him soon," DC Morrison assured her. "Half the Devon police force is looking for him. He won't get far."

After he left, we gathered our things slowly, none of us eager to venture out into the night with a confessed killer on the loose.

"You should both stay at the cottage tonight," I said to Freya and Beau. "I don't think any of us should be alone."

"I'm definitely not going up to my flat tonight," Freya said with a shudder. "Not after knowing Colin was creeping around the building earlier."

We walked home through the village, both dogs on high alert. The normally peaceful streets felt different, menacing somehow. Every shadow could be hiding someone, every sound might be footsteps. Hardy kept close to my legs while Austen swept the area ahead with her watchful gaze.

The cottage felt wonderfully safe when we finally got inside. I turned on all the lights, checked the locks twice, and put the kettle on for yet more tea. Sometimes, in times of crisis, tea really was the answer.

"I'm in the guest room," Beau said with his characteristic Southern courtesy. "Freya, you should take it. I'll be perfectly comfortable on the sofa."

"I couldn't possibly—" Freya started.

"I insist," Beau said firmly. "My mother would never forgive me if she knew I'd taken a bed while ladies slept on couches."

"Well, when you put it that way," Freya said with a small smile. "Thank you."

As we were settling in with yet another pot of tea, Malcolm would be proud of our consumption rate, someone knocked at the door. Both dogs immediately went into protection mode, growling low. Through the peephole, I could see Elliot standing on my doorstep, looking concerned. He was wearing his emergency call-out clothes, the waterproof jacket and boots he wore for nighttime veterinary emergencies.

"I heard what happened," he said when I opened the door. "The whole village is talking about it. Are you all right?"

"We're fine," I said, touched by his concern. "Just processing everything. Come in, we've got tea on."

Elliot stepped inside, greeting both dogs who immediately relaxed at his familiar presence. His gaze swept the cozy domestic scene, Beau arranging pillows on the sofa, Freya curled up in the armchair with a blanket, me in my most comfortable cardigan. Something flickered in his expression when he noticed Beau's obvious familiarity with my cottage.

"Quite the gathering," Elliot observed, his tone carefully neutral.

"Safety in numbers," Beau replied, equally neutral, though I caught the slight edge of Southern politeness that meant he was marking territory.

"The police are everywhere," Elliot continued, accepting the mug of tea I offered while positioning himself on the opposite side of the room from Beau. "They've got boats searching the harbor, dogs on the coastal path. It's like something from a television drama."

"Except it's real," Freya said, apparently oblivious to the

subtle tension between the two men. "Colin really killed Gary, and now he's out there somewhere."

We settled in the living room, the curtains drawn against the night. It felt like we were in a bubble of warmth and light while chaos unfolded outside. Hardy claimed his spot on the hearth rug while Austen positioned herself where she could watch both the front door and window.

"I keep thinking," Elliot said slowly, sipping his tea, "about where Colin might go. He doesn't know the area well. He's only been here for the fair."

"The police are checking the obvious places," Beau said, stretching his legs in a way that subtly claimed more space in my small living room. "The train station, the harbor, the main roads out of town."

"But what if he's not trying to leave?" I suggested, refilling everyone's cups from the pot. The familiar ritual of pouring tea helped steady my nerves. "What if he's hiding somewhere, waiting for things to calm down?"

"Where would he hide?" Freya asked, pulling her blanket tighter around herself. "He doesn't know anyone here except the people from the fair."

Hardy had settled at my feet, occasionally lifting his head to check that everyone was where they should be, while Austen maintained her post by the window, ears swiveling at every distant sound.

"You know," Elliot said thoughtfully, shifting his chair slightly closer to mine, "there are places he would have seen during the fair. The venues for workshops and readings."

"The village hall is swarming with police," I said. "But what about the old museum building? Angela held that creative writing session there on Friday."

"Worth checking," Beau agreed, though he seemed more focused on the way Elliot had moved closer to me. "And there's that Victorian greenhouse behind the manor house. Didn't someone do a nature writing workshop there?"

"Marcus Webb," Freya remembered. "Said the atmosphere was perfect for inspiration."

"Then there's the fisherman's cottage where the historical society met," Elliot added. "Diana did an atmospheric writing workshop there on Saturday. Colin would have been there."

"Three places to check," I said. "We should tell DI Drake."

I tried calling, but it went straight to voicemail. The police were probably overwhelmed with the search.

"We could go check ourselves," Elliot suggested carefully. "Just to see if he's there. If he is, we call the police immediately."

"That's a terrible idea," Beau said firmly, his protective instincts clearly activated. "DI Drake specifically told Ginny to stay inside and lock the doors."

The way he said it, emphasizing his concern for me specifically, made Elliot's jaw tighten slightly.

"But what if he's there and he's..." I paused, not wanting to voice the possibility. "What if he meant something else by 'putting his affairs in order'?"

The phrase hung in the air, heavy with implication.

"We're not seriously considering going after a murderer in the middle of the night?" Freya asked.

"We'd just check," Elliot said. "From a safe distance. If we see any sign of him, we call the police and leave."

"This is insane," Beau muttered, but I could see him wavering.

Through the window, we could see torch beams in the distance as police searched the harbor area. They were focused on escape routes, not hiding places.

"We should at least try calling DI Drake again," I said, dialing the number once more. Still voicemail.

"Look," Elliot said, "I'll go check myself. You all stay here—"

"Absolutely not," I interrupted. "If anyone's going, we all go. Safety in numbers."

"This is how people in mystery novels get themselves killed," Freya pointed out, but she was already reaching for her coat.

Both dogs had picked up on our energy, moving toward the door with alert anticipation. Hardy's tail was low, all business, while Austen watched us intently, picking up on the serious mood.

"We're really doing this?" Beau asked.

"Just a quick check," I said, though even I didn't quite believe it. "If he's not there, we come straight home. If he is, we call the police and wait for them to arrive."

As we prepared to leave, I noticed the familiar signs of a village crisis pulling together. Mrs. Patterson's lights were on next door, and I could see her peering through her curtains. Across the lane, the Weatherbys had their porch light on, the universal village sign for "we're awake and watching."

"At least if something happens to us, there'll be witnesses," Freya said with dark humor.

"Nothing's going to happen," Elliot said firmly. "We're just going to look."

But as we stepped out into the night, I couldn't shake the feeling that we were about to do something incredibly foolish. The village felt different in the darkness, familiar landmarks transformed into ominous shadows. Somewhere out there, Colin Mitchell was running or hiding, desperate and dangerous.

And we were about to go looking for him.

"The old museum is closest," Elliot said quietly. "Just five minutes if we take the back lanes, avoid the main police search areas."

"This is such a bad idea," Beau muttered, but he fell into step beside me.

Hardy and Austen flanked us, alert and watchful. They knew something serious was happening, and they were ready to protect their humans from whatever danger lay ahead.

As we made our way through the darkened village, I could hear the distant sounds of the official search—shouts, whistles, the drone of a helicopter somewhere over the water. The police were pulling out all the stops to find Colin.

But what if we were right? What if he wasn't running at all, but hiding in one of the places that held some connection to his weekend at the fair?

The old museum was waiting somewhere in the darkness ahead. And despite every sensible part of my brain screaming warnings, we were walking straight toward it.

———

22

The back lanes of Tidehaven Cove were barely wide enough for two people to walk side by side, bordered by high stone walls covered in ivy that rustled mysteriously in the night breeze. Our footsteps seemed unnaturally loud on the cobblestones, despite our attempts to walk quietly. Hardy and Austen moved silently beside us, their usual clicking claws muffled by centuries of moss growth between the stones.

The scent of night-blooming jasmine drifted from someone's garden, mixing with the salt air from the harbor. It should have been pleasant, but knowing a killer was loose somewhere in these familiar streets made everything feel sinister.

The museum was really just a converted Georgian house that held local artifacts and dusty displays about smuggling history. We crept around to the back where Angela had held her creative writing workshop, using the conservatory for "inspiration from the past."

Elliot tried the door. Locked, as expected. Through the windows, we could see nothing but darkness and the vague shapes of display cases. Hardy sniffed along the foundation with professional thoroughness while Austen kept watch.

"Nothing," Elliot concluded after peering through several windows. "No signs of forced entry either."

"One down," Beau said, staying close to my other side in a way that created an almost competitive flanking formation with Elliot.

We continued through the narrow lanes, passing cottage windows glowing with warm lamplight. Through one, I could see Mrs. Whitmore knitting in her parlor, her cat curled on her lap. Such normal, cozy scenes while we hunted for a murderer.

As we rounded the corner near the bakery, dark now, but still emanating the faint smell of tomorrow's bread already rising, a figure suddenly lurched out of the shadows.

"Bloody hell!" a familiar voice exclaimed.

We all jumped, Freya letting out a small shriek. Hardy and Austen issued low growls.

It was Oliver Blackthorn, balanced precariously on crutches, his leg in a cast that gleamed white in the darkness.

"Oliver!" I gasped, heart still racing. "What are you doing out here?"

"I could ask you the same thing," he said irritably, trying to maintain his dignity despite nearly falling over. "Can't a man go to his own shop to check the damage without being accosted by roving gangs?"

"Your shop is a crime scene," Beau pointed out reasonably. "And you're supposed to be missing."

"I've been in hospital in Cardiff," Oliver said with exaggerated patience, as if we were particularly slow children. "Broke my leg examining a Victorian escritoire. Spectacular piece, actually, mahogany with ivory inlay. Worth the fall, almost."

"You fell downstairs looking at furniture?" Freya asked.

"The seller failed to mention the third step was rotted through," Oliver grumbled. "Three days in a Welsh hospital with no phone—it broke in the fall—eating appalling food and listening to the man in the next bed describe his bowel troubles in excruciating detail."

Despite everything, I found myself fighting back a laugh. Even in the middle of a manhunt, Oliver's complaints were oddly comforting.

"Have you seen Colin Mitchell?" Elliot asked. "He's the one who killed Gary."

"The romance writer?" Oliver's eyebrows shot up. "Good lord. Though now that I think about it, he was asking rather specific questions about the fisherman's cottage after that workshop on Saturday. Wanted to know if smugglers really used it, whether anyone ever hid there successfully from the authorities."

Elliot and I exchanged glances. That seemed significant.

"We should check there," I said.

"You should go home and let the police do their job," Oliver corrected firmly. "And I should go home before this blasted cast gets any wetter. The damp is seeping through already."

He hobbled off toward his house, muttering about murder on his Persian rug and insurance companies that would "undoubtedly find a way to avoid paying for biological fluid damage."

"Only Oliver would worry about insurance forms while there's a manhunt," Freya said, but fondly.

"Should we follow Oliver's tip and go straight to the cottage?" Beau asked.

"No," I said, thinking it through. "Colin might have realized Oliver could tell someone about his questions. Let's stick with our plan, check the greenhouse first, then the cottage."

The Victorian greenhouse stood behind Thornfield Manor, now converted to luxury flats but with the grounds preserved as a community garden. The greenhouse itself was a beautiful structure of iron and glass, though many panes were cracked or missing.

We approached through the herb garden, the scent of crushed thyme and rosemary rising where we stepped on the overgrown path. The greenhouse door stood slightly ajar.

"Someone's been here," Elliot whispered.

We crept closer, torches off to avoid giving away our position. Inside, moonlight filtered through the broken panes, creating a patchwork of light and shadow among the abandoned plant benches and broken pottery.

"Colin?" I called softly.

A cat—not Captain but one of his many relatives—shot out from behind a potting bench, making us all jump again. Freya grabbed my arm, and I noticed both men moved protectively closer.

"My heart can't take much more of this," Beau said, his voice shaky.

After thoroughly searching the greenhouse and finding nothing but spiders and that indignant cat, we headed toward our final destination, the fisherman's cottage on the cliff path.

The cottage sat alone on its promontory, dark against the star-filled sky. But as we approached, both dogs stopped, hackles raised. And then we saw it. A faint flicker of light in one of the windows.

"He's there," Freya whispered.

Before Beau could call the police, the cottage door opened and Colin stood silhouetted against the dim light from within.

"I wondered when someone would think to look here," he called, his voice carrying clearly across the distance. "The clever bookshop owner and her entourage. Though I didn't expect quite so many of you."

My heart was pounding, but I tried to keep my voice steady. "Colin, the police are looking for you. You should turn yourself in."

"Should I?" He laughed bitterly. "So I can spend the rest of my life in prison? A romance writer who killed someone over a manuscript. The tabloids will have a field day."

"You don't have to make this worse," Elliot said in his calm, veterinary voice, the one he used with frightened animals. "Come back with us peacefully. We'll call DI Drake, and you can surrender without any more drama."

"Peacefully," Colin repeated with a bitter laugh. "There's no peace for me now."

He retreated into the cottage, leaving the door open. Hardy pulled free and raced toward it, barking urgently, with Austen right behind adding her voice to the alarm. Without thinking, I ran after them.

"Ginny, no!" Both men called simultaneously, which might have been funny in other circumstances.

Inside, Colin stood by the fireplace where a small fire burned. He was feeding pages into the flames—his manuscript. The cottage smelled of woodsmoke and damp, with that particular mustiness of buildings too close to the sea.

"Don't," I said. "That's all you have left of what the book should have been."

Colin paused, a page in his hand. "Does it matter? Who's going to want to read a book by a murderer?"

"The work exists separate from what you've done," I said, stepping carefully over the uneven flagstone floor. The dogs stayed close, protective but not aggressive, their barking having subsided to watchful alertness.

Behind me, I heard Elliot and Beau entering, Freya calling the police from the doorway.

"It's over anyway," Colin said, feeding another page to the fire. "I can't run forever. I don't even want to. I just... I needed to see it burn. To know that no one else could corrupt it."

"Colin," Elliot said gently, "you're not thinking clearly. This won't solve anything—"

"Nothing will solve anything!" Colin laughed harshly. "I'm a murderer. That's all anyone will ever see now."

Through the window, we could see blue lights approaching along the cliff path.

"They're coming," Colin said unnecessarily. He looked at the remaining pages in his hands, then set them down on the dusty mantle. "Maybe someone else can make something of them. Someone who isn't a killer."

Within minutes, DI Drake's team had surrounded the cottage. Colin walked out with his hands raised, surrendering without resistance. As they led him away in handcuffs, he looked back once at the cottage, then at me.

"Look after the pages," he said quietly. "They deserved better than what happened to them."

DI Drake approached us with a face like thunder. "Ms. Hampton, Dr. Harrington, Mr. Morrison, and Ms. Collins, what part of 'stay inside and lock your doors' was unclear?"

"We tried to call," I said weakly.

"So you decided to confront a confessed killer on your

own?" Her voice was dangerously quiet. "Do you have any idea how foolish that was?"

"Yes," we all said simultaneously.

She stared at us for a long moment, then sighed. "You found him, at least. And no one got hurt. But if you ever do something this foolish again..." She let the threat hang.

"We won't," I promised, though I suspected she didn't believe me.

As we were escorted back to the village by a rather annoyed police constable, I looked back at the fisherman's cottage. Colin's manuscript pages were still on the mantle, waiting for someone to decide their fate.

"That was incredibly stupid," Elliot said as we walked, but his hand briefly touched my shoulder in concern.

"Monumentally stupid," Beau agreed, moving to my other side.

"Never doing that again," Freya added firmly.

The walk home was quiet except for our footsteps and the distant sound of police radios. The village looked different now, familiar streets and cottages transformed back into the cozy place I knew, the danger having passed with Colin's arrest.

"I think we need something stronger than tea," I suggested as we reached the cottage. "I've got sherry in the cabinet, the good stuff Malcolm insists I keep for 'medicinal purposes.'"

"Oh, yes," Freya said with feeling.

"Medicinal purposes sounds exactly right," Elliot agreed.

Inside, I poured generous measures of sherry into the good glasses while everyone collapsed into chairs, the adrenaline finally wearing off. Hardy and Austen did their rounds, checking that everyone was safe before settling down with satisfied sighs.

"To surviving our own stupidity," Beau raised his glass.

"To never doing that again," Freya added.

"To Colin's manuscript," I said quietly. "May it finally rest in peace."

We drank in companionable silence, the warmth of the sherry and the familiar comfort of my cottage gradually replacing the cold fear of the night's adventure. Through the window, we could still see occasional police lights in the distance, but here in our little circle of lamplight, with the dogs at our feet and sherry warming our insides, we were safe.

"I should probably head home," Elliot said eventually, though he made no move to leave.

"I'd offer you the sofa," I said, "but I'm afraid it's already spoken for."

I caught the quick glance between the two men; the subtle tension over territory and proximity.

"I should check on my own animals anyway," Elliot said diplomatically. "But thank you."

As he left, he squeezed my hand briefly. "I'm glad you're safe."

After he'd gone, Beau helped me clear the glasses while Freya headed upstairs, exhausted.

"That was brave of you," he said quietly. "Stupid, but brave."

"I couldn't let Colin destroy everything," I replied. "Not the manuscript, not himself."

"I know." He paused at the bottom of the stairs. "That's one of the things I've always admired about you, Ginny. You can't help but try to save everyone."

Before I could respond, he'd headed to the sofa, leaving me to wonder about the implications of "always admired" and the way both men had been so protective tonight.

23

Wednesday morning arrived with heavy rain that hammered the cottage windows and turned the garden into a muddy lake. Hardy stood at the back door, looked at the weather, and gave me the most reproachful look a corgi could manage.

"I know," I told him. "But you need to go out."

Austen trotted past him into the downpour, did her business efficiently, and returned to shake herself off on the kitchen mat. Hardy followed with obvious reluctance, managing to look tragic despite being outside for less than thirty seconds.

The cottage still showed evidence of last night's drama. Empty sherry glasses on the coffee table, Beau's pillow and blanket neatly folded on the sofa, Freya's shoes kicked off by the door. The everyday mess that proved life continued after extraordinary events.

"Morning," Beau said, emerging from the living room already dressed and looking far too put-together for someone who'd slept on a sofa. "Coffee or tea?"

"Tea," I said automatically. "Always tea in a crisis."

"Is it still a crisis?" He filled the kettle clearly at home in my kitchen. "I thought we'd moved on to the aftermath stage."

Freya stumbled down the stairs, her hair sticking up at impossible angles. "Please tell me someone's making tea. I can't face reality without tea."

"Kettle's on," Beau assured her.

We gathered around the kitchen table, warming our hands on our mugs while the rain pounded against the windows, washing the village clean of last night's drama. Hardy had positioned himself on my feet, his way of forgiving me for the wet garden incident, while Austen nosed their food dishes around hoping I'd forget filling them a short while ago.

"The shop," I said suddenly. "Malcolm will be wondering what happened."

"Malcolm knows everything," Freya said, scrolling through her phone. "The village WhatsApp group has been going since dawn. Mrs. Patterson saw us with the police last night and... oh dear."

"What?"

"She's started a collection for our 'trauma.' Apparently Elspeth's organizing counseling tea and cakes at the tea shop this afternoon."

"Counseling tea?" Beau looked puzzled.

"It's like regular tea but with more sympathy and possibly some of Elspeth's emergency bourbon cake," I explained. "She served it last month after a rather severe storm."

The phone rang, startling all of us. I hoped we'd all settle down soon, being so jumpy was hard on the nerves.

"Ginny?" DI Drake sounded tired but considerably warmer than during last night's scolding. "Wanted to update you. Colin Mitchell's given a full confession. He also told us to check his laptop. There's a file with dated drafts going back two years that proves he wrote the original. Though with his confession, it's all rather moot."

"How is he?" I asked, remembering his desperation at the cottage.

"Under psychiatric observation. He'd taken sleeping pills with alcohol before you found him. If you'd been any later..." She paused. "Well, your stubbornness saved his life."

My stomach clenched. We'd been right about his plans.

"Oh, and Oliver Blackthorn filed a complaint about being accosted by vigilantes. He withdrew it when we explained how you'd contributed to the capture, and his attitude might look petty. He wanted it 'on record' that his injury recovery was disrupted."

"That sounds exactly like Oliver."

After I hung up and shared the news, we sat quietly for a moment, processing the near-tragedy we'd prevented.

"Right," Beau said, breaking the silence. "Time to face the world?"

The walk to the bookshop was soggy but somehow cleansing. The heavy rain had washed the streets clean, and the village looked fresh and ordinary, as if murders were something that happened in books, not in real life.

Malcolm had already opened the shop and was arranging a display of crime novels with obvious satisfaction.

"Miss Hampton! Thank goodness. The entire village has been asking about you." He gestured toward the back room where I could smell fresh tea brewing. "I've prepared provisions."

Not just tea, but a plate of what looked like Mrs. Patterson's homemade shortbread and some of Elspeth's breakfast sandwiches.

"Malcolm, you didn't have to—"

"Nonsense. After the night you've had, proper refreshments are essential." He actually smiled, a rare occurrence. "Besides, we've sold seventeen mysteries this morning already. Apparently authentic murder scenes are good for business."

Captain appeared from behind the poetry section, gave us all a dismissive look that suggested we'd disrupted his morning routine, and settled into a sunny spot that had just appeared as the clouds broke.

The shop bell chimed and Elliot rushed in, wearing his veterinary jacket and looking concerned.

"Between calls," he said. "Just wanted to check you were all holding up after last night. That was quite an ordeal."

"We're fine," I assured him, noting how Beau had subtly moved closer to me.

"You saved Colin's life." Elliot's grey eyes were serious. "That was brave."

"That was stupid," I corrected. "But lucky."

"Both," Beau said from where he'd stationed himself by the new releases. "Most heroic acts are."

The two men exchanged one of their looks—not quite hostile, but definitely measuring.

"I have to run," Elliot said. "Mrs. Henderson's cat won't vaccinate itself. But later, maybe dinner? To properly celebrate everyone surviving?"

"That would be nice," I said, catching Beau's slight frown.

After Elliot left, the shop felt smaller somehow.

"When's your flight?" I asked Beau, trying to sound

casual while rearranging books that didn't need rear-ranging.

"Friday." He paused. "Unless there's a reason to change it."

Before I could figure out how to respond to that loaded comment, Diana Hartwell swept through the door with Priya in tow, both carrying takeaway coffee cups from Elspeth's.

"Darling Ginny!" Diana enveloped me in a cloud of expensive perfume and genuine warmth. "We're leaving today but I couldn't go without thanking you. The delightful Elspeth has been singing your praises at the tea shop, apparently you've solved murders before? You've become quite the detective!"

"I mostly just stumbled around in the dark," I protested.

"With excellent results," Diana said firmly. "DI Drake mentioned you'd saved Colin's manuscript, the real one, not Gary's mangled version. That was good of you."

"The literary world is buzzing," Priya added, bouncing slightly with excitement. "Romance writer murders thriller writer over stolen manuscript. You couldn't make it up!"

They left with promises of lunch in London and hints about a television producer interested in the story, which made me slightly queasy.

The morning brought a steady parade of villagers, some buying books, others just wanting to hear about our midnight adventure firsthand. Malcolm handled them all with surprising grace, managing to turn curiosity into sales with remarkable efficiency.

"Seventeen mysteries this morning," he announced with satisfaction. "Twenty-three if you count the advance orders."

Sarah Pemberton arrived just before lunch, impeccable

despite the weather in a Burberry raincoat that probably cost more than three months' rent in Charleston.

"Despite the unfortunate murder," she said crisply, "I've signed two new clients from the workshops. So professionally speaking, a success."

She left her card "in case you ever write about your adventures" which made Beau laugh.

"You should," he said. "You've got enough material."

"I run a bookshop," I reminded him. "I don't write books."

"Yet," Freya said, then looked innocent when I glared at her.

Oliver arrived after lunch, maneuvering his crutches through the door with considerable cursing.

"Fingerprint powder," he announced without preamble. "Do you know what that does to Persian rugs? And the insurance forms!" He collapsed into Malcolm's chair with a theatrical sigh. "Forty-seven pages. Forty-seven! For one murder!"

"Tea?" Malcolm offered, apparently deciding Oliver qualified as trauma-adjacent.

"Please. And perhaps some of that shortbread, if you can spare it."

As Oliver complained about insurance companies, crime scene cleanup services, and the general inconvenience of having murders in one's shop, I noticed the village returning to its rhythm. The rain had finally stopped, weak sunshine was breaking through, and life in Tidehaven Cove was reasserting its cozy normalcy.

"You've done something special here," Beau said quietly, appearing at my elbow while Oliver regaled Malcolm with insurance horror stories. "This place, these people—they've claimed you."

"Or I've claimed them," I said, watching Freya teach Oliver how to balance a teacup while on crutches.

"Maybe both."

Hardy had settled on the hearth rug, content in his domain, while Austen maintained her watchful position by the door. The shop smelled of tea and old books. Customers came and went, buying mysteries and leaving gossip. Captain stretched in his sunny spot, supremely indifferent to human drama.

"So," Beau said, his Southern accent more pronounced, "about Friday..."

But before he could continue, Hardy decided it was definitely time for his afternoon walk, and some conversations, I realized, would have to wait. We'd had enough life-changing moments this week.

The ordinary pleasure of walking dogs in damp Devon lanes felt like exactly what we all needed.

24

I stood at the cottage window with my first cup of tea, watching Mrs. Patterson's roses drip with last night's rain while Hardy and Austen investigated the garden with renewed enthusiasm.

"Beautiful morning," Beau observed, joining me at the window with his own mug. He was already mostly packed, his leather bag sitting by the door like a countdown timer. Tomorrow he'd be gone.

"It is," I agreed, trying not to think about his departure.

Freya had already left for her flat. "I need clean clothes that don't smell like adventure," she'd said—leaving Beau and me alone in my kitchen. The morning sun streamed through the windows, Captain the cat had appeared from wherever he spent his nights to claim a sunny spot on the windowsill, and everything felt deceptively peaceful.

"What's the plan for today?" he asked.

"Normal bookshop things, hopefully. Malcolm's probably already there, maintaining standards and terrorizing the poetry section into alphabetical submission."

"No more murders to solve? No more manuscripts to save?"

"Good lord, I hope not. I just want to sell books and drink tea and pretend the most exciting thing in my life is whether to stock more Agatha Christie."

But when we arrived at the shop, it was clear that normal was still some distance away. A small crowd had gathered outside, and Oliver was holding court from his position on crutches, apparently giving an impromptu tour.

"...and it was right there," he was saying, pointing through the window, "where that dreadful man met his unfortunate end. On my nineteenth-century Amritsar rug, which I'll never look at the same way again."

"Oliver," I said, "what are you doing?"

"Damage mitigation," he replied without embarrassment. "If people are going to gawk, they might as well learn about the historical significance of my collection. Did you know that rug once belonged to a maharaja's third wife?"

"I did not," I said, unlocking the bookshop door. "But perhaps we could move the historical lecture away from the murder scene?"

"It's not a murder scene anymore," Oliver corrected. "It's a commercial space with a fascinating past and a slight depreciation in value due to unfortunate circumstances."

Once inside, I watched Oliver settle into the comfortable chair near the mysteries section with obvious satisfaction. It occurred to me that he was making himself quite at home in my shop, almost as if he already owned it, which he most certainly did not and never would if I had anything to say about it.

Malcolm had indeed already arrived and was arranging a new display. Books to Die For featured prominently, which seemed both inappropriate and commercially savvy.

"Malcolm," I said, "isn't that a bit..."

"Topical?" he suggested with a perfectly straight face. "I thought so. We've had three phone calls already this morning from people wanting to reserve copies of anything similar to Colin's situation."

"That's morbid."

"That's commerce," Malcolm corrected, though I caught the slight upturn of his lips that passed for amusement.

The morning proceeded with surreal normalcy. Customers came and went, some genuinely interested in books, others clearly hoping for gossip or a glimpse of something murderous. Oliver continued his residency in the mystery chair, regaling anyone who'd listen with increasingly elaborate stories about his furniture and the insurance industry.

Around eleven, Elliot appeared with a small box from the bakery.

"Peace offering," he said, setting it on the counter. "For dragging you into danger the other night."

"You didn't drag me anywhere," I protested. "I dragged myself. And everyone else."

"Still." He glanced around the shop, noting Beau's absence. "Where's your house guest?"

"At the tea shop," I said. "Elspeth cornered him about our midnight adventure. He may never escape."

"About tomorrow," Elliot said, suddenly intent on studying the pastry box. "I know your friend is leaving. I wondered if you might like dinner? Somewhere that doesn't involve chasing murderers or discussing manuscripts?"

Before I could respond, Beau walked in carrying a tray of takeaway coffees from Elspeth's.

"Thought everyone could use a mid-morning boost," he said cheerfully, though his eyes narrowed slightly at Elliot's presence. "Elspeth sends her regards and about seventeen questions about Tuesday night."

"Only seventeen?" I said. "She's showing restraint."

The two men stood on opposite sides of the counter like some sort of romantic standoff in a bookshop. Hardy looked between them with interest, while Austen maintained her position by the door with diplomatic neutrality.

"I should go," Elliot said. "Surgery this afternoon. But think about dinner tomorrow?"

After he left, Beau set down the tray with unnecessary precision.

"Dinner tomorrow," he said. "That's nice. Very... prompt."

"Beau—"

"No, it's good. You should have dinner. With the local vet. Who lives here. In your village. Where you live." Each statement came with careful emphasis.

"Are you jealous?"

"Of course not. Why would I be jealous? Just because I'm leaving tomorrow and he's already making plans doesn't mean..." He stopped, apparently hearing himself. "I'm jealous."

The words triggered a memory of Charleston, of Beau choosing his career over us, of me watching him leave. We'd had our chance and he hadn't taken it. But maybe it just hadn't been the right time. Maybe neither of us had been ready then.

"I know. Doesn't mean I have to like watching someone else step into the space I vacated."

Before this could become a proper conversation about feelings and history, Diana's assistant Priya burst through the door, looking frazzled.

"Thank God you're open," she said. "Diana needs me to

check something urgently. She's had an offer from a publisher, a substantial one, for a book about the whole Gary and Colin situation. She wanted to make sure you were serious yesterday about not wanting to write about it yourself."

"Completely serious," I assured her. "I have no interest in turning this tragedy into entertainment."

"I might," Oliver piped up from his chair. "Could be rather diverting while I convalesce. 'Murder at the Literary Fair: An Insider's Account.' Has a ring to it, doesn't it?"

Priya looked uncertain. "I'll... tell Diana that's a possibility. Also, she wanted me to mention that she's now Colin's literary executor. Romance writers often designate someone to handle their literary estate. Diana offers it as a professional service. She and Colin had an arrangement."

"That makes sense," I said. "What will happen to his manuscript?"

"She's thinking of trying to get the original published under his name, with proceeds going to a literacy charity. Something good from all this mess."

After Priya left, the shop felt quieter. Oliver had dozed off in the chair, snoring gently. Malcolm was helping a customer find the perfect birthday gift. Captain had relocated from my cottage windowsill to claim a sunny spot on the poetry section and was grooming himself with regal indifference.

"Walk?" Beau suggested, and both dogs immediately went on alert.

We headed toward the harbor, taking the long route through the village. The crime scene tape was gone from Oliver's shop, the police cars had vanished, and Tidehaven Cove looked exactly as it had before the fair, peaceful, pretty, and decidedly unmurderous.

"I've been thinking," Beau said as we walked. "About Charleston. About here. About choices."

"And?"

"And I don't have any answers. Just... possibilities."

We'd reached the harbor, where fishing boats bobbed in the afternoon sun. Hardy was investigating some particularly interesting seaweed while Austen had spotted the gulls and was barking enthusiastically, jumping and trying to chase them despite being on her lead.

"Austen, enough," I said, though I was laughing at her determination. "You're never going to catch them."

"I could come back," Beau said suddenly. "Not permanently, not yet, but... to visit. See if there's something here worth changing my life for."

"Is there?" I asked calmly, though my heart was racing.

"I don't know. That's what I'd need to find out." He turned to face me. "Would that be something you'd want? Me coming back?"

Before I could answer, Hardy decided to shake himself off, spraying us both with seawater and effectively ending the moment.

"Typical," Beau laughed, wiping his face. "Even your dog has timing issues."

We walked back to the shop, the question hanging between us. I found myself thinking about his offer. Yes, there was still something between us, that was obvious. But there was Elliot too, steady and already part of this life I'd built. Though if I was honest, he'd been friendly but not exactly pursuing me with great passion. Maybe dinner tomorrow would clarify things. Or maybe it would just complicate them further.

The afternoon brought Marcus Webb, looking better than he had in days.

"I wanted to thank you," he said. "For solving this before it destroyed the entire literary community. I've been absolutely shattered by the stress of it all. Being suspected of murder is not conducive to editorial work, I can tell you. I'm only now starting to feel like I can return to my actual life."

"I didn't really solve anything," I protested.

"You saved Colin's life and his manuscript," Marcus corrected. "That's more than solving—that's redemption. And now I can go back to worrying about normal things like print runs and review copies instead of whether people think I'm a killer."

As the day wore on, I realized the village was already incorporating this latest murder into its mythology. By next year, the story would have grown and changed, becoming part of Tidehaven Cove's narrative alongside smuggling tales and ghostly fishermen.

"You know what?" I said to Malcolm as we closed up. "Maybe we should do the fair again next year."

Malcolm looked at me as if I'd suggested burning books.

"Without the murder," I added.

"One would hope," he said dryly. "Though at this rate, we should probably add 'potential crime scene' to our insurance coverage."

That evening, Beau and I had dinner at the pub, nothing fancy, just fish and chips and local ale, while Hardy and Austen waited hopefully under the table for dropped chips. The pub was warm and noisy, filled with locals discussing everything from the weather to the murder, and I realized how much this place had become home.

"This is nice," Beau said. "Normal. No one's confessing to murder or stealing manuscripts."

"Just chips and beer and dogs," I agreed.

"And possibilities," he added, raising his glass.

"And possibilities," I echoed.

25

F riday morning arrived too quickly, bringing Beau's departure. Today the weather turned misty, not raining but not clear, turning everything into a farewell scene from a wartime romance. I stood in the cottage kitchen, breathing in the comforting smell of toast and scrambled eggs, while rain pattered gently against the windows. Beau checked his pockets for the third time, making sure he had his passport, tickets, and phone.

"You don't have to drive me to the station," he said again.

"I want to," I replied, scrambling eggs while Hardy and Austen positioned themselves strategically by our feet, ready to pounce on any dropped morsels. The kitchen was warm and steamy from cooking, the windows fogging up around the edges. "Besides, the dogs need a proper run, and the fields near the station are perfect."

We ate breakfast in comfortable silence, both pretending this was just another morning. The cottage felt different knowing he was leaving, emptier somehow, even though he was still sitting right there spreading Elspeth's homemade marmalade on his toast very slowly, as if he could stop time with each careful stroke of the knife. Somewhere outside, Mrs. Patterson's rooster announced the morning despite the late hour.

"I'll wash up," he offered when we'd finished.

"Leave them. We need to go or you'll miss your train."

The drive to the station took us through the village one last time. The rain had stopped, leaving everything fresh and gleaming. We passed the bookshop where Malcolm was already arranging the window display, the warm glow of lights making it look like a haven. The tea shop's windows were steamed up, and I could see Elspeth's shadow moving about inside, setting out her morning pastries. The smell of fresh bread from the bakery followed us down the street.

"It's a good place," Beau said quietly. "I can see why you love it here."

At the station, we stood on the platform while the dogs investigated the interesting smells around the bench. The mist was lifting, revealing glimpses of the green hills beyond. The station's hanging baskets dripped with last night's rain, and the old wooden waiting room sign creaked in the breeze.

"So," Beau said, setting down his bag.

"So," I agreed.

"I meant what I said about coming back. This doesn't have to be goodbye forever."

"I know."

The train appeared around the bend with a rumble and hiss, and suddenly there wasn't enough time for all the things we hadn't said.

"Ginny," he started, but I shook my head.

"Not now. Not like this. If you come back, we'll talk then. When there's time to do it properly."

He kissed my cheek, a gentle gesture that somehow felt

more intimate than anything else might have. "Take care of yourself. Try not to find any more bodies."

"I'll do my best."

He boarded the train, found his seat by the window, and waved as it pulled away. Hardy and Austen sat perfectly still beside me, watching the train disappear into the morning mist.

"Come on, you two," I said finally. "Let's go home."

But instead of heading straight back to the cottage, I drove to the bookshop. I needed the comfort of familiar surroundings and Malcolm's predictable presence.

The shop bell chimed cheerfully as I entered, and the familiar smell of old books, leather bindings, and Malcolm's lavender furniture polish wrapped around me like a hug.

"You're early," Malcolm observed from behind the register. "Mr. Morrison catch his train?"

"Yes."

"Ah." Malcolm busied himself with the tea service, the delicate clink of china his way of offering comfort without the burden of words. "Miss Collins called. She's bringing pastries from the bakery."

"Of course she is."

The morning passed quietly with its comforting routines. The kettle whistled, customers came and went with the gentle chime of the door bell, buying their Friday reads for the weekend. Mrs. Patterson stopped by to gossip about the murder "aftermath," as she called it, and to buy the latest gardening magazine, trailing the scent of her rose perfume. Captain claimed his usual spot in a patch of morning sun and regarded everyone with benign indifference, occasionally stretching luxuriously to maintain optimal warmth.

Around eleven, my phone buzzed with a text from Elliot: "Still on for dinner? 7 pm at the Harbour Inn?"

I'd completely forgotten about dinner in the emotion of Beau's departure.

"Yes," I texted back. "Looking forward to it."

Was I? I wasn't sure. Everything felt unsettled, like a book with pages out of order.

"You look thoughtful," Freya said, appearing with the promised box of pastries, the sweet smell of cinnamon and sugar following her in. "Post-departure blues?"

"Something like that."

"He'll be back," she said confidently, helping herself to a chocolate croissant that left flakes all over Malcolm's carefully maintained counter. "I saw the way he looked at you. And the way he looked at Elliot. That's not a man who's giving up."

"It's complicated."

"The best things usually are." She licked chocolate from her fingers. "Speaking of which, Oliver's been in his shop since dawn with industrial cleaners, muttering about biological contamination and insurance deductibles. Mrs. Patterson says she could hear him shouting instructions from across the green."

"Life goes on," I said.

"It does," Malcolm agreed, appearing with fresh tea in the good china. "And speaking of which, I've had three calls this morning about next year's literary fair. Apparently, despite the murder, or perhaps because of it, people are very interested in attending."

"We're not having another murder," I said firmly.

"Well, one would hope not," Malcolm replied, the corner of his mouth twitching. "Though at the rate we're going, we should perhaps consider it as a unique selling point."

The afternoon brought Diana Hartwell, making a surprise return visit, her perfume preceding her into the shop like an expensive announcement.

"I know I said goodbye yesterday," she said, sweeping in with her usual dramatic flair, "but I had to come back. I've been reading Colin's original manuscript, the undamaged parts, and it's genuinely good. With some editing and restoration work, it could be published."

"That's wonderful," I said, meaning it.

"I've spoken to his solicitor. Colin's royalties will go to his mother initially, but she wants to donate them to a literacy charity after taking care of his legal fees." Diana paused. "It's all terribly sad, but at least something positive might come from it."

"What about Gary? Does he have family?"

"A sister in Manchester. She's arranged for a quiet cremation. Apparently, they weren't close, but she said she wasn't surprised by how things ended. 'Gary always did make enemies easier than friends,' she told me when I called to offer my sympathies."

After Diana left in a cloud of good intentions, the shop felt quieter. The afternoon sun slanted through the windows, creating pools of golden light that Captain systematically moved through, maintaining optimal warmth. The old radiator ticked peacefully, and I could hear Freya humming as she shelved returns.

"I should probably go home and change for dinner," I said eventually.

"Ah yes, Dr. Harrington," Malcolm said with careful neutrality. "He's very reliable."

"Reliable," I repeated. "What every woman dreams of hearing."

"I merely meant he's already part of village life. Established. Present." Malcolm paused, adjusting his bow tie. "Unlike some people."

"Beau might come back."

"Perhaps. But Dr. Harrington is here now."

It was a fair point, even if it wasn't entirely what my heart wanted to hear.

At home, I made myself a cup of tea and carried it upstairs, the dogs following hopefully. The cottage was filled with early evening light, golden and warm. I stood in front of my wardrobe trying to decide what to wear. The dogs watched from the bed, occasionally offering helpful suggestions in the form of tail wags when I held up different options.

"The blue dress?" I asked them. Hardy's tail thumped approval against the quilt. "You're right, nice but not too formal."

I settled on the blue dress with a cardigan, elegant but still practical for a Devon evening. The dogs watched me apply lipstick with great interest, as if this deviation from routine was worth monitoring.

The Harbour Inn was everything a proper village pub should be, warm and welcoming, full of Friday night locals and the smell of good food. A fire crackled in the inglenook fireplace despite the mild evening, and the low-beamed ceiling created intimate pockets of light and shadow. The familiar sounds of clinking glasses, laughter, and the fruit machine's occasional jingle made it feel like stepping into a warm embrace.

Elliot was already there, standing when he saw me approach, looking rather handsome in a way I hadn't quite noticed before. He'd traded his usual veterinary fleece for a proper shirt and jacket.

"You look lovely," he said, pulling out my chair.

"Thank you. You clean up rather well yourself when you're not covered in pet hair."

He laughed, and I realized I'd never really heard him properly laugh before. It was nice, warm and genuine.

We ordered, fish pie for me, the Inn's was legendary, steak for him, and started talking about the village, but quickly moved beyond small talk. Our corner table was perfectly positioned, close enough to the fire to be cozy but far enough from the bar to talk properly.

"I have a confession," Elliot said, pouring us both wine from the bottle of red he'd chosen. "I was jealous of Beau all week. The history you two have, the way you look at each other sometimes."

"Elliot..."

"Let me finish," he said gently. "I was jealous, but I also realized something. I've been so careful around you, so worried about not pushing too hard after everything you've been through, inheriting the shop, the murders, adjusting to village life, that I forgot to actually show you who I am."

"What do you mean?"

"I mean I've been playing it safe. Being the helpful village vet who's there when you need him but never really letting you see that I'm interested in more than just being helpful." He met my eyes directly. "I'd like to change that, if you're willing."

I found myself really looking at him for perhaps the first time. Not just as Elliot-the-vet who'd helped with the dogs and joined our midnight manhunt, but as a man who was intelligent, kind, and actually quite attractive when he wasn't being carefully professional.

"I'm still confused about Beau," I admitted.

"I know. And that's okay. I'm not asking you to choose right now, or to make any grand declarations." He smiled.

"I'm just asking if we could actually get to know each other. Properly. Not as the village vet and the bookshop owner who solve murders together, but as Elliot and Ginny."

"I'd like that," I heard myself saying, and was surprised to find I meant it.

The rest of dinner felt different, lighter somehow. Our food arrived steaming and delicious, and we talked about books. He was a secret science fiction fan, travel, he'd spent a year working with wildlife in Africa, and his terrible attempts at cooking, apparently he once set pasta on fire, which should be physically impossible.

"I had no idea you were funny," I said, laughing at his story about chasing an escaped parrot through the village while wearing only one shoe, still in his pajamas.

"I'm full of surprises," he said. "For instance, I play jazz piano rather badly, I'm terrified of butterflies for no logical reason, and I think your dog Hardy might be smarter than both of us combined."

"Hardy is definitely smarter than me," I agreed. "He never would have chased a murderer through the village at midnight."

"But that's what I like about you," Elliot said. "You do the unexpected. You care enough to do the stupid, brave thing."

After dinner, he walked me home through the village. The mist had cleared, leaving a sharp, clear night full of stars. The village was settling into its nighttime rhythm, televisions glowing through curtained windows, the smell of woodsmoke from chimneys, and a man singing as he walked along the street.

"This was nice," I said at my door, the porch light casting a warm glow. "Different than I expected."

"Good different?"

"Yes. Definitely good different."

He leaned in and kissed me. Not on the cheek like Beau had, but properly. It was warm and surprising and rather lovely.

"Too soon?" he asked, pulling back.

"No," I said, surprised by my own response. "Just unexpected."

"Good. I plan to be unexpected more often." He smiled. "Can I see you again? Tomorrow?"

"I'd like that."

Inside, Hardy and Austen greeted me with enthusiasm, as if I'd been gone for days rather than hours. The cottage was warm and welcoming, the lamp I'd left on creating a pool of light in the living room.

"Well," I told them as I put the kettle on for evening tea, "that was interesting."

My phone buzzed. A text from Beau: "Landed safely. Charleston feels different. Missing Devon already. Missing you."

I stared at the message for a long moment, then typed back: "The dogs miss you too."

Another buzz: "Just the dogs?"

I hesitated, thinking about the evening with Elliot, about Beau being far away, about choices and timing and complications.

"Not just the dogs," I typed finally. "But things are complicated here."

"Complicated how?"

How could I explain that I'd just had a lovely evening with Elliot? That I'd felt something I hadn't expected? That my heart was somehow pulled in two directions?

"Just complicated. We should talk when you visit."

"I'm still planning to come back next month. If that's okay."

"It's okay. We need to talk properly."

"Ginny, is there hope for us?"

I looked at the phone for a long time before typing: "Maybe. I don't know. That's part of what's complicated."

There was a long pause before his response: "I see. Well, I suppose I deserve that. I'll still come visit if you want."

"I want you to. We need to figure out what we are to each other."

"Fair enough. Get some rest. Give the dogs my love."

I put the phone down and looked around my cottage, my safe, cozy cottage with its creaking floorboards and rattling windows, in my safe, cozy village where life was becoming increasingly complex. The tea kettle whistled, and I made my evening cuppa in my favorite mug, the one with painted roses around the rim that somehow made it more perfect.

In four weeks, Beau would be back, and we'd have to face whatever was still between us. But tomorrow, I was seeing Elliot again, and that felt right too.

"Come on," I told the dogs, settling into my favorite chair with my tea and a biscuit. "Let's pretend everything's simple."

26

Three weeks later, I stood in the middle of Hampton Books watching Malcolm glare at the new computer terminal as if it had personally insulted his mother. The familiar smell of old books and Malcolm's lavender furniture polish surrounded us, but even these comforting scents couldn't soften his expression of betrayal.

"I fail to see," he said stiffly, "why a perfectly functional system that has served us admirably for decades needs to be replaced with this... contraption."

The morning light streaming through our front windows caught the dust motes dancing above the new equipment, making everything look slightly magical despite Malcolm's technological resistance. I could hear Freya typing enthusiastically at her laptop setup near the poetry section, the rhythmic clicking providing counterpoint to Malcolm's complaints.

"Because the old till doesn't connect to our inventory system," Freya explained patiently, not looking up from her screen. "And because customers expect to pay with cards, and because we need to track stock levels automatically instead of..."

"Instead of using a proper ledger and human intelligence," Malcolm finished stiffly, adjusting his bow tie. "Yes, you've made your position clear."

I bit back a smile while demonstrating the card reader for the third time, the familiar weight of the small device oddly reassuring in my hands. "Malcolm, it's really quite simple. The customer inserts their card here, enters their PIN—"

"What if they don't have a PIN? What if the machine breaks? What if there's a power cut?" Malcolm had clearly been lying awake at night cataloguing every possible technological failure. "What happens to commerce then?"

"We still have the manual card machine as backup," I assured him, gesturing toward the drawer where we kept the old sliding contraption. "And cash, obviously."

"Obviously," he repeated with deep skepticism.

Both dogs were sprawled on the hearth rug, watching our technological drama with mild interest. Hardy occasionally lifted his head when Malcolm's voice rose, while Austen had positioned herself where she could keep an eye on both the front door and our activities. Captain, lazing in his usual sunny spot and was studiously ignoring all of us, occasionally stretching one paw into a particularly warm patch of morning sunlight.

"Look," Freya said, turning her laptop screen to show us the basic online shop framework, "I've got the main categories set up—Fiction, Non-Fiction, Local Interest, Children's. We can add inventory as we go, starting with new releases and special orders. The videos we made reading to kids are on here too."

"Online sales," Malcolm muttered, as if Freya had

suggested selling books from a cart on the moon. "What's next? Robots delivering books by drone?"

"Actually," Freya said with dangerous enthusiasm, "there are some fascinating developments in automated—"

"No," I interrupted quickly, the sharp scent of fresh tea from Malcolm's morning pot reminding me that some traditions were worth preserving. "Let's master the card reader before we revolutionize publishing."

The shop bell chimed with its familiar brass voice, providing a welcome distraction from our technological struggles. Oliver maneuvered through the door on his crutches, his messenger bag slung awkwardly across his shoulder beneath his jacket. He looked considerably more cheerful than the last time we'd seen him, his cast now decorated with what appeared to be small sketches of antique furniture drawn in different colored inks. The rubber tips of his crutches squeaked slightly on our old wooden floor as he made his way to Malcolm's favorite reading chair.

"Ginny!" he called, settling into the worn leather with obvious satisfaction. The chair creaked under his weight. "Just the person I wanted to see. I have a proposition."

"Should I be worried?" I asked, noting how both dogs immediately focused on Oliver with alert interest.

"Not at all. It's a business proposal of mutual benefit." He arranged his crutches carefully beside the chair, the metal gleaming in the morning light. "I've been thinking about sustainable tourism for our region. Literary tourism, specifically."

"Go on," I said cautiously.

"Well, we can't always count on dramatic events to draw the crowds," Oliver continued, choosing his words carefully.

"But we could offer combined literary and historical tours. Your bookshop expertise paired with my knowledge of local history and antiques."

Malcolm looked up from the card reader with obvious interest, his earlier technological frustrations momentarily forgotten. "Literary tours?"

"Exactly. 'Books and Bygones of South Devon', guided walks featuring literary connections, historical sites, perhaps ending with cream tea and book browsing." Oliver's voice took on the enthusiasm of someone warming to a favored topic. "I've already identified seventeen points of interest, including the cottage where that minor Victorian novelist spent a summer, the pub where they say smugglers planned their routes, and naturally, both our establishments."

"That's actually quite clever," Freya said, abandoning her laptop setup. "Literary tourism is huge. People love feeling connected to books and authors."

I found myself genuinely intrigued despite my suspicions about Oliver's motives. "What sort of partnership were you thinking?"

"I handle the historical elements, you provide literary context, we split the tour fees." Oliver's proposal sounded reasonable, but I caught the calculating gleam in his eyes. The same look he got when examining a piece he suspected might be worth more than the seller realized. "Of course, we'd need to coordinate our business operations closely. Very closely. Perhaps even consider some sort of... merger of interests."

"Merger," I repeated carefully, my fingers unconsciously tightening around the card reader.

"Well, naturally, if we're going to be business partners, it would make sense to streamline our operations. Reduce overhead. Perhaps consolidate our retail spaces into one larger, more efficient—"

"Oliver," I interrupted, "are you trying to buy my book-shop again?"

"Not buy," he said with wounded innocence that would have been more convincing if he hadn't been mentally measuring our shelf space. "Partnership. Joint venture. Mutual expansion of complementary businesses."

Malcolm snorted with what might have been amuse-ment, the sound mixing with the gentle hiss of the tea kettle in the back room. "Mr. Blackthorn, you are nothing if not persistent."

"I prefer 'strategically minded'," Oliver replied with dignity. "Though I admit the shop acquisition would be a natural evolution of our partnership."

"The tours sound interesting," I said, setting down the card reader with a soft click. "The merger, not so much."

"Well, we could start with the tours and see how things develop," Oliver said, clearly not giving up on the larger scheme. "I've already prepared some sample itineraries."

He opened his messenger bag and withdrew a thick folder, the papers rustling softly in the quiet shop. The folder was one of those expensive leather ones with brass corners that looked like it belonged in a Victorian solicitor's office—very Oliver. He showed me detailed maps of the region with marked stops, historical notes, and even suggested reading lists. I could smell the faint scent of expensive paper and see Oliver's meticulous handwriting in the margins, apparently his organizational skills were unimpaired by crutches.

"You've put a lot of work into this," I admitted, genuinely impressed despite myself. The maps were hand-drawn with artistic flourishes, and someone had clearly spent hours researching historical details.

"I've had nothing but time since that unfortunate incident with the furniture authentication and the rotted stair," Oliver said, shifting slightly in the chair to ease his cast into a more comfortable position.

"What kind of tours were you imagining?" Freya asked, clearly caught up in the possibilities, her fingers already tapping against her laptop as if planning digital marketing campaigns.

"Several options. 'Smugglers and Stories' focusing on the more colorful aspects of local history. 'Gardens and Gothic' for the literary ladies who enjoy atmospheric settings. 'Maritime Mysteries' combining fishing heritage with crime writing." Oliver consulted his notes. "'Cozy Crimes and Cream Teas' for the murder mystery enthusiasts."

"Given our recent experiences," I said, thinking of Colin's confession in this very shop, "that last one might be a bit too authentic."

"That's exactly what would make it popular," Oliver countered, his eyes bright with commercial enthusiasm. "We could even include the actual locations. My shop, your bookshop, the fisherman's cottage. Properly presented, of course."

Malcolm looked appalled, his bow tie practically quivering with indignation. "You want to turn our recent trauma into tourist entertainment?"

"I want to turn our local assets into sustainable income," Oliver corrected. "And yes, that includes our recent notoriety. People are fascinated by real crime. We might as well benefit from their fascination."

I had to admit there was a certain logic to it, even if it felt slightly ghoulish.

"Literary expertise, book recommendations, author anecdotes. You know more about books and reading than anyone in the village." Oliver paused, studying my expression. "Plus, you've actually solved murders. That gives you credibility in the crime tourism market."

"I didn't solve anything," I protested, feeling heat rise in my cheeks. "I just stumbled around until things became clear."

"Modesty," Oliver said dismissively, waving one hand while balancing his folder with the other. "Tourists love modesty. Makes them feel superior while still being impressed."

Before I could respond to this dubious compliment, the new card reader emitted a triumphant beep. Malcolm had successfully processed a dummy transaction, and his expression of surprise was worth documenting.

"Well," he said, blinking at the small screen, "that was... not entirely terrible."

"See?" Freya said encouragingly. "Technology isn't the enemy."

"Technology is a tool," Malcolm corrected with his usual precision, though I caught the hint of grudging acceptance in his tone. "Whether it's an enemy or ally depends entirely on the competence of those wielding it."

"Speaking of competence," Oliver said, clearly sensing an opportunity to advance his agenda, "I should mention that I've already contacted the tourism board about our tour concept. They're very interested. Apparently, literary tourism brings in visitors who spend more money and stay longer than average tourists."

"You contacted the tourism board without asking me?" I said, feeling the first stirrings of irritation prickle along my spine like static electricity.

"I mentioned it as a possibility," Oliver backtracked smoothly, though his expression suggested he'd done considerably more than mention it. "Pending your agreement, naturally. Though they did say they'd love to feature it in their summer brochures if we can launch by spring."

I looked around the bookshop—my bookshop, with its familiar creaks and comfortable corners, which Oliver was clearly still plotting to acquire through this partnership scheme. But the tour idea did have merit, and it would bring more customers to both our businesses.

"I'm interested in the tours," I said finally, my words carrying the weight of careful decision. "But I'm not interested in any business mergers, acquisitions, or hostile takeovers disguised as partnerships."

"Hostile takeovers," Oliver repeated with theatrical hurt, pressing one hand to his chest. "As if I would ever—"

"You offered to buy the shop the day I inherited it," I reminded him, the memory still sharp despite the months that had passed.

"That was different. That was a straightforward business proposal. This is creative collaboration."

"This is creative collaboration that you hope will lead to a business acquisition," I said, meeting his gaze directly.

"Well," Oliver admitted, "eventually. But there's no harm in starting with tours and seeing how we work together."

Freya was practically bouncing with excitement, her earlier laptop work forgotten. "We could create special book bundles for tour participants! Local interest titles, crime novels, maybe some signed copies from visiting authors!"

"And I could provide historical context for the antiques and architecture," Oliver added, warming to the collaborative possibilities. "Plus, I do have the most authentic period costumes in the village."

"Period costumes?" Malcolm inquired with interest, his technological trauma apparently forgotten in favor of this more appealing development.

"For atmospheric effect. Nothing too elaborate, just enough to enhance the historical experience." Oliver's eyes gleamed with the prospect of theatrical presentation.

I found myself imagining Oliver in Georgian dress leading a group of tourists through the village, and had to admit it would be quite charming. If I could keep him from using the tours as a pretext to gradually absorb my business.

"All right," I said, the words coming out before I could second-guess myself. "Let's try a trial run. One tour, to see how it works."

"Excellent!" Oliver beamed, pulling out what appeared to be a detailed timeline from his folder. The papers rustled with the satisfaction of plans coming to fruition. "I was thinking we could start with 'Cozy Crimes and Cream Teas' since we have the most material for that theme."

"Of course you were thinking that," I said dryly, though I couldn't suppress a small smile. "What if I'd said no to the whole idea?" I asked, realizing how much he'd already committed to this venture.

"Then I'd have had to find another charming bookshop owner with a talent for solving mysteries," Oliver said smoothly. "Though I doubt I'd find one quite so conveniently located."

I calculated quickly in my head. Next weekend would be cutting it close to Beau's planned visit, but the tour should be finished well before his train arrived. "Next weekend it is, then," I said, surprising myself. "One trial run."

"Saturday afternoon, two o'clock. Elspeth's already prepared special menus for the cream tea finale." He maneuvered his crutches toward the door, the rubber tips squeaking rhythmically against our floor. "Don't worry, if this goes well, we'll be booked solid through next summer season."

The afternoon brought a steady stream of customers, several of whom were delighted to discover they could now tap their cards or use their phones to pay. The soft electronic beeps of successful transactions provided a modern counterpoint to the shop's traditional atmosphere. Malcolm handled the new technology with increasing confidence, though he still muttered about the superiority of ledgers and human memory.

Oliver returned just before closing time, carrying a second, even thicker folder of tour materials.

"Background reading," he said. "Crime locations, historical context, suggested talking points. I thought you might want to review everything before our trial run."

After he left, I spread the contents of his folders across the counter, breathing in the scent of fresh photocopying and Oliver's expensive paper stock. The man had been incredibly thorough—maps, photographs, historical timelines, even a suggested script for the tour narrative. I could feel Malcolm and Freya peering over my shoulders, their curiosity making the space feel crowded in a comfortable way.

"He's certainly prepared," Malcolm observed, picking up one of the maps.

"Too prepared," I said, running my fingers along the edge of a particularly detailed map. "It doesn't make me any less sure this is all part of an elaborate scheme to get his foot in the door." The paper felt expensive under my fingertips, the kind Oliver would choose for maximum impact.

"Probably," Freya agreed cheerfully, the laptop keys clicking as she continued her online shop setup. "But the tours could be brilliant for business. And you can always say no to any merger attempts."

I picked up one of Oliver's maps, noting how he'd marked the bookshop as a "key literary landmark" and included detailed information about its history and current operations. Even the font he'd chosen looked official, as if this were already an established business venture rather than a trial run.

"We'll see," I said, gathering up Oliver's materials. The papers rustled satisfyingly as I stacked them. "One tour. If he behaves himself and doesn't try to acquire anything, we might have a real partnership."

"And if he doesn't behave?" Malcolm asked, his tone suggesting he already knew the answer.

"Then I'll set Austen on him," I said, though I was only half joking.

Book and History tours sound peaceful. Well, until a body shows up. Grab your copy of Poison and Prose today to join Ginny on her next case.
Click Here

Claim your copy of The Charleston Diary when you sign up for my newsletter. Learn how Ginny solved a case of forgery before she headed to the peace and tranquility of Tidehaven Cove.

CLICK HERE

If you enjoyed reading Bound by Secrets please consider helping other readers to find the story by leaving a review.

CLICK HERE

WANT MORE

∾

Book and History tours sound peaceful. Well, until a body shows up. Use the QR code below to grab your copy of Poison and Prose today to join Ginny on her next case.

∾

If you enjoyed reading Bound by Secrets please consider

helping other readers to find the story by using the QR code to leave a review.

ABOUT POPPY BRIDGEMAN

Hi, I'm Poppy Bridgeman, the cozy mystery alter ego of Canadian author P A Wilson. Poppy was "born" because sometimes stories need a gentler touch—with a little magic, a dash of humor, and plenty of sleuthing spirit.

As Poppy, I write the *Witch of Henbane Island* series (where witches and festivals collide with mysteries), the *EB Eats Culinary Mysteries* (a small-town diner, a determined heroine, and murder on the menu), and the *Pages & Paws Bookstore Mysteries* (a Devon bookshop, two mischievous corgis, and plenty of secrets tucked between the shelves).

When I'm not tangled in my characters' escapades, I'm happily tangled in yarn—I knit, weave, and doodle in sketchbooks between writing sessions. I also love to travel, finding inspiration for charming settings, quirky characters, and suspicious strangers wherever I go.

Home base is the Vancouver area, where I juggle writing as both Poppy and P A Wilson. Whichever name is on the cover, I'm always chasing the next story.

ALSO BY POPPY

For more books by Poppy Bridgeman

scan the QR code below.

FREE BOOK

Claim your copy of The Charleston Diary when you sign up for my newsletter. Learn how Ginny solved a case of forgery before she headed to the peace and tranquility of Tidehaven Cove.

ACKNOWLEDGMENTS

People think that the process of writing is solitary. That's not the case for me. I have help from so many people it would be hard to acknowledge everyone, but I'll give it a try.

The support and inspiration I get from my writer's groups is incalculable. The Vancouver Writers Social Group opens my mind to other ways of telling a story. The Royal City Literary Arts Society gives me the opportunity to meet and share with other writers who have more knowledge than I do. The Other 11 Months group is where I learn about getting the words on the page. And my critique group who helps me find the best parts of the story I want to tell. Thanks to all of the members of these great groups.

Last of all, but definitely a huge part of the process, my beta readers. These are the people who love stories and are willing, and more than able, to tell me if my finished story is ready for you, my readers.